LETHAL GAME

BEARS UNDER SIEGE

A SAM TRAVIS ADVENTURE
BOOK ONE

GK JURRENS

WITH
LT. TOM KASPRZAK (RETIRED)

UpLife
Press

eBook ISBN: 978-1-952165-25-2
Paperback ISBN: 978-1-952165-26-9
v.221115_1415
r.23071723_0937
GKJurrens.com

---

*Please note the list of major characters
in the appendix.*

DISCLAIMER

Although this tale is based on a true story, this is a work of fiction. Any similarity to actual persons, behaviors, places or events should be considered coincidental and fictional.

No part of this publication may be stored in a retrieval system, transmitted, or reproduced in any way, including, but not limited to, digital copying and printing without prior agreement and written permission of the publisher, UpLife Press.

Research of this manuscript's period and its theme mandated judicious use of ethnic pejoratives and mild profanity, and are not meant to offend the reader. Quite the contrary, the use of these literary devices is intended to demonstrate the authentic commitment to a higher set of moral standards and to the strength of each character's faith, or lack thereof.

DEDICATION

To all who need to hear Tom's story.

ACKNOWLEDGMENTS

To my friend, Tom Kasprzak
and to all my beta readers and technical advisors.
I thank you for being part of the team.

And Tom wishes to thank the eighty-nine male and female environmental officers from seven states that participated in the takedown of the bad guys during *Operation Berkshire,* the massive joint effort that spanned almost three years to thwart an illegal wildlife harvesting ring across seven states and two countries. They arrested twenty-nine criminals and achieved an incredible 99.9% conviction rate.

A special thanks to Captain Larry Johnson and the late Officer Emmett "Jack" Dickman, both of the Massachusetts Environmental Police, and Investigator Steven Canfield of the New York Environmental Conservation Police.

INTRODUCTION

"Lethal Game" is based on a true story, adapted from a screenplay written by Lieutenant Tom Kasprzak of the Massachusetts Environmental Police.

Unauthorized hunting of animals is commonly referred to as *poaching*. Those who disobey might hunt before or after the legal hunting season or use an illegal weapon to hunt a particular species. Such offenses may be unwitting.

Or these poachers could be ruthless criminals seeking to profit from the immoral killing of wildlife en masse, sometimes resulting in the extinction of an entire species.

Even worse, the illegal wildlife trafficking industry is estimated in the billions. Its consequences can be seen in the tragedy of countless animal carcasses. Some international authorities even attribute trillions in illicit gains to such enterprises.

Criminals harvest and traffic parts of wild animals—often just small but valuable parts of their bodies—and they leave the bulk of the animals to rot where they're dropped.

With so much money at stake, such a criminal enterprise attracts unscrupulous individuals who will stop at nothing to satisfy their heinous greed.

And there are some who just love to kill.

Within the Commonwealth of Massachusetts, Environmental Police Officers (EPOs) are much more than game wardens. It is their duty to investigate violations and enforce all state statutes regarding firearms, hunting, fishing, motor vehicles on highways and byways, as well as all-terrain vehicles, snowmobiles and boats.

Like many criminal enterprises, loss of human life is also inevitable.

This is one such story of two EPOs enforcing the law and seeking justice. Or vengeance.

PROLOGUE

AUGUST, 1988

Wonju, Gangwon Province

South Korea

A DENSE FOG STUNK LIKE WET WOOL—DANK AND THICK. Sagging strings of colored lights that hung low over the narrow street painted halos in the drifting mist; that is, those bulbs that weren't burned out or shattered. The late afternoon sun almost failed to shine through the clouds, fog and exhaust fumes.

The boy was accustomed to the pungent stench that always saturated this neighborhood. It stung his nostrils and irritated his sensitive eyes. But the urchin's enthusiasm was hard to miss even in the poor visibility. His was to be an important task for an important man—someone everyone called *Uncle*. This could lead to more jobs.

I won't be hungry anymore. Not tomorrow, anyway.

The skinny pre-teen splashed through the oily surface of a shallow puddle. Around a dark corner into an even darker alley from the narrow cobbled street, there hunched *Uncle*. That wrinkled old man drew on the long pipe in the corner of his mouth at the pharmacy's alley entrance.

The venerable old herbalist shook his head as if impatient or angry, probably both. The boy could not see Uncle's right hand as he clasped it behind him. Mad little puffs arose from his long, curved ivory pipe cradled in the crook of his crippled left hand.

The boy slid and stumbled from his dead run. The street was oily slick and littered with wet newspaper pages of yesterday's trivia. He bumped into Uncle, who stumbled back into the closed door with a soft grunt.

The boy mumbled, "Sorry, Uncle."

He looked up at the craggy face, then dropped his chin to his chest. Too close. He had invaded this important man's personal space. He shuffled back a pace under that icy stare.

Uncle's chest-length beard stunk of curry and...

flowers? No, that was opium. Uncle was a rich man. He was not to be disrespected. The boy stepped back yet another pace, bowed, brought his hands together in front of his lowered face as if praying, but his eyes turned upward, pleading for leniency. He needed this job.

The venerable old man said, "You are late, Han, and you are careless."

"*Please* forgive me, Uncle." Han bowed again for good measure. The old gentleman swept one arm from behind. In his upturned palm, he revealed a small package wrapped in gold foil. With a ceremonial flourish and his pipe now clenched in between his few remaining teeth, he placed the package the size of a large pea into a small box just large enough —maybe one inch square.

"Yes, hurry, now. Hyung Gang Wa will reward you well."

ALWAYS JITTERY WHEN WITHIN THE OLD PHARMACIST'S presence, young Han was in awe of the stinky old man. The kid snatched the box now containing the gold-wrapped pea, and offered one last bow, little more than a quick head bob. Han bolted for the mouth of the alley and the safety of the street.

The sky opened. Rain in Wonju always tasted

metallic at first. Something from the factory. Han's feet were already mud-splattered, anyway. Just that when his sandals got wet, they stretched. Cheap leather, *but* he was proud they *were* leather. Made running harder and tripping easier.

He protected the little gray box containing the gold pea from the rain with his body. Surely, it shouldn't get wet. Uncle hadn't said.

As Han ran, the streets grew wider and straighter. Cleaner, too. Not that Uncle lived in a poor part of town, mind you, but Hyung Gang Wa was *very* rich.

There it was. The bathhouse. So much white—pillars, fancy statues.... Men with money always loved big and white and fancy.

I wonder if that is true everywhere, or only in Wonju.

He had been nowhere else.

Now, Japanese and American cars filled the boulevard. He dodged each of them with ease as he crossed four lanes of traffic between manicured gingko trees shedding their autumnal colors in the median. He cursed as he stepped on a piece of their stinky fruit scattered on the grass. As he crossed the southbound lanes, the shouts of angry drivers who slammed on their brakes bombarded him with words and gestures of a most profane nature. They leaned on their horns.

Trees on both sides of the street and in the median dripped with the heavy raindrops that pummeled Han's stubbled head.

As he got closer to the bathhouse, he admired the cornucopia of white statues resting on its manicured front lawn behind wrought iron.

HAN STOPPED. HE KNEW HE WAS LATE, BUT UNCLE HAD told him what he carried was important. Tempted to peek at what was inside the gold foil within the little box, he resisted. Could be fatal.

He paused, then scrambled up the white wooden steps leading to the front door. Breathing hard, he knocked, waited, knocked again. The massive portal cracked open. The suspicious eyes of the huge muscular attendant flashed recognition. Swung the door open enough for his important torso to pass through to the covered landing.

Han dropped the package into the monster's outstretched right hand. It was massive. Han leaned left around the big man's tree-trunk body as the package disappeared into a pocket. He tried to sneak a look at the women inside.

The monster grabbed a fistful of Han's sturdy

shirt with his left hand, raising him three feet off the white wooden landing outside the bathhouse's tall doors. The tree trunk sneered and said, "Curiosity is for cats. That can get them killed."

He slapped Han's face with such force the boy's head snapped to his right and back. Blood dripped from his nose onto both his shirt and the attendant's left hand that still held him suspended. Tree Trunk appeared both amused and angry. Laughing, he flung Han down the stairs, along with a few coins that scattered in every direction.

The bathhouse attendant shouted to Han where he lay. "Watch your manners, boy! And one day the honorable Hyung Gang Wa might invite you in. Now go!"

Face down in the puddle nearer the cobbled street, Han smiled. Tree Trunk could not see his grin. A small toss down a few stairs was well worth a fistful of coins. He could tell from their jangling as he fell this was already a profitable day. Yes, he would eat.

Han picked himself up, wiped his nose and gathered every coin before scampering off. That big man always tipped better when he got to toss Han down those stairs. A little game. Han would thank Uncle for the work on the way home.

He'd hope to catch another sweet whiff of Uncle's opium pipe.

INSIDE THE BATHHOUSE, NEARLY NAKED WOMEN AND MEN lounged in dreamy contentment. A gray sun shone through skylights and reflected off tiled pools of tepid water. Exotic vapors fanned upward toward the twenty-foot teakwood ceiling.

Several of Hyung Gang Wa's customers lay on their backs atop several cushioned tables that lined the walls around the blue-tiled pool. Their bellies glistened as women applied various lotions and oils to arouse them.

A macabre carnival revolved through the big attendant's mind. The reflected light off the wavy water, the steam, the oils, incense and flaccid nudity, along with the sounds of happy endings now and then.... The big man grinned with his head on a swivel as he walked. His job was the best in the world.

He approached an oak-paneled door. Turned the knob. It squeaked. He winced. Entered Hyung Gang Wa's private chamber with the gold-wrapped package in his hand.

Large ornate carvings of wooden lions and

dragons peered down from all four corners of the ceiling. A threadbare red rug covered the floor except for the three feet of glossy bamboo planks around its perimeter. Dozens of candles flickered and offered a sensual glow.

TRANSLUCENT CURTAINS DOTTED WITH SILVERY BEADS veiled the four-posted bed. Tendrils of incense within rose toward the bed's mirrored overhead in the dim light, where reflections of three full-breasted girls tangled with Hyung Gang Wa's oiled body—a mass of obese flesh.

The attendant drew near, bowed to the tall woman in a lacy gown who stood guard next to the bed. She tried to take the package, but Tree Trunk insisted on handing it over to his master himself.

The woman cleared her throat to gain her master's attention and parted the curtain. The attendant refused to back away under the tall woman's fierce gaze. He filled his eyes and nostrils with the revolting yet stimulating sight of the fat man trying to have fun.

The tall woman awaited the right moment as the three young girls continued to massage Hyung Gang Wa from his shiny scalp to the soles of his corpulent feet. He yawned. They escalated their movements, both in speed and intensity. The attendant failed to appear disinterested. The big man yawned again despite their steady manipulations.

Now noticing the gauzy veil had parted, Hyung Gang Wa jerked away from the trio of teenage girls whose breasts were too big for their age. He bolted upright, his face waxen, eyes heavy-lidded.

The morbidly obese man's voice gurgled and rasped as he spoke. "What has kept you?"

Tree Trunk said, "The boy was late."

"I'll have the pharmacist's head if it happens again." He extended a soft, plump hand. "Well, the package, you idiot. Give it here, quickly. Quickly!"

The attendant nodded, saying nothing, handed the gold pea over with a deferential bow. He then rushed from the room with visions of the three young maidens burned into his libido.

———

HYUNG GANG WA'S PUFFY EYES FLASHED WITH desperation. Removed the gold foil. Popped the gray-white nugget into his jowled mouth. He swallowed without benefit of water or his ever-present cup of rice wine.

Two of the girls rubbed his back. The third employed her attention elsewhere. He leaned forward and sighed, revealing his yellow teeth and larger-than-life dimples in both jowled cheeks that pressed upward toward his adipose-encased eyes, they were little more than foggy slits.

A moment later, his enthusiasm swelled. The girls responded with fingers now exploring below his waist with slow rhythmic motions at first. Then, more vigorously. The fat man's smile grew wider and wider.

1

THE TOWN'S PRINCIPAL THOROUGHFARE SCREAMED *QUAINT*.

Its small stores and steepled churches looked like a Norman Rockwell painting. Farmhouses, barns, and fenced-in pastures normally as green as emeralds clustered around Wedgewood.

From above, a proud sun dappled grassy meadows through millions of gold, brown and yellow leaves that had been a dozen shades of brilliant green just a few weeks earlier. These meadows peeked out from folds in the earth like wrinkles in a blanket on a crisp and sunny day. In and around Wedgewood and its rolling hills, all seemed beautiful, serene, perfect.

A rusty Ford Bronco rumbled down a country road. The official state seals on the Bronco's doors announced this old four-wheel-drive truck belonged to the Massachusetts Environmental Police.

Sam Travis hunched behind the wheel listening to the strains of Robert Palmer's *Simply Irresistible* on the radio, and tapped his thumbs to the beat on the wheel. His threadbare uniform was a bit small these days. He wore it pressed—with pride. Well, sort of. He didn't not *love* his job, but could imagine doing nothing else. Naw, he was made for this gig. But there were days....

The Bronco rambled up the sloping driveway, stirring up the dust that was an artifact of this autumn's dry weather. Oak and birch trees stood at attention on either side of the curved drive, but they looked tired. He'd stacked three cords of dried oak, beech and white birch alongside the left end of the cape-style house weeks ago. Most of it was ready to generate some heat. The house's weathered cedar shakes and shingles held in that heat during cold winters.

Travis's heart fluttered. The Bronco's door creaked as he swung it open. The heady scent of pine sap all around the yard reminded him why he loved living out here. As he slid out of the truck, the tip of his holster always dragged on the seat to his right. The protruding hammer had long since worn a hole in the seat's back.

Patched with the wrong-colored vinyl repair tape, allegedly permanent—he just called it duct tape—was already peeling off. Travis swore he'd get his tired ass to a junkyard to find another seat. He'd scavenge another old truck to butcher. On behalf of the Commonwealth of Massachusetts, of course.

But that would take time he didn't have. Maybe he'd just wander down to Hank's hardware store. He'd find a suitable seat cover with elastic straps to hold it in place, and to hide the hole... at least to keep it from getting worse.

He checked the new leather retainer loop he'd had sewn into his old holster. Secure. Kept his trusty old revolver from falling out. A reflex. Time and weather had loosened that holster, but it was part of him. The old .357 Smith and Wesson sported too many scratches in its finish from dropping to the ground as he'd crawled out of that old truck the last couple of years. The gun showed some battle scars but was meticulously maintained. His life had too often depended on it.

Travis frowned at the grass growing up and

around his old lawnmower in the front yard. Plus, most of a pile of garden hose was not visible in the tall grass—a.k.a. weeds. A rake leaned against the house, and the damn weeds held that old rake hostage, too, growing right through its blades. He'd take a day off....

SAM'S FROWN OF GUILT TURNED INTO A GRIN. SPOTTED Brian, his twelve-year-old son, bottle-feeding a scrawny fawn he cuddled in his arms at the bottom of the porch's steps. Poachers had slaughtered the tiny deer's mom. Kind of how cancer slaughtered his own. They had adopted "Fawny"—Brian had named her.

This kid.

"Hi, kiddo. School let out early?"

Brian said, "Hey, Dad. Kinda."

"Waddaya mean, kinda?"

"I didn't know if you could make it in time to feed him," he nodded down at the little deer, "so I excused myself from the last period."

Travis stared down with clamped lips and one cheek puckered. After a shallow sigh of resignation, he said, "Excused? You mean skipped, don't you?"

"Jeez , Dad. It's not that." Brian wrinkled his forehead as if his next words were the most sincere he ever uttered. "Just trying to keep her goin' after all she's been through. We don't want to lose her now, do we?"

Travis hinted at a grin as the boy looked up at him, ruffled his son's hair as he climbed the first porch step.

"Okay. But remember, schoolwork comes first." He took a deep, cleansing breath. "Getting big, isn't she?"

"Yeah. Must be the vitamins."

Travis climbed the rest of the steps at a tired pace.

2

THESE WOODS ALWAYS REMINDED FRANK MURDOCK OF Christmas. The pine and hemlock trees that loomed over the log cabin stained its brownish exterior to somewhere between a weathered gray and the black of neglect. But it always smelled like Christmas.

Out front, a sign nailed to a post announced,

Environmental Police
Regional Headquarters,
Glenville, Mass.

Frank swung open the cabin's screen door. It banged against its stops as he stepped out onto the porch and filled his lungs. Sometimes he felt stronger than he himself expected. The truth? He had grown too darn old and tired for the job. But he'd admit that to no one out loud, not even to himself.

He slapped away the cobwebs from the top corner of the screen door. They weren't there last night. A few clung to the sergeant's stripes on his right shoulder. Those stripes were less faded than the rest of his forest-green uniform. He scratched at the third-day stubble on his jowled neck.

The grizzled game service veteran hobbled side-to-side out to his Bronco, a clone of the one that his partner, the promising young Sam Travis drove, though rustier. But for the sweet fart of fate, he'd have lost one or more of that truck's Swiss cheese fenders behind him in a ditch on a country road.

His left knee gave him trouble most of the time. Today was one of those days. Not the only thing that irritated him, though.

These dents and all this grime? Past adventures, eh? If we get some budget, maybe the boss springs for a new fleet of Broncs... yeah, sure thing—come a hell a Sundays!

Frank grabbed the handle, swung open the

driver's door with a screech from its pair of rust-dry hinges and hoisted his creaky carcass up into the driver's seat. His eyes had grown bloodshot from filling out forms for the last hour.

Blasted paperwork...two more years and I'm gone... gone... gone....

Twisted the ignition key.

Bam!

The Bronco sputtered and stalled. Murdock slammed his fist against the wheel. The muscles in his jaw rippled. Didn't mean to grind every single natural tooth left in his mouth. Probably chipped at least one, or worse. He was sure to put the dentist's youngest boy through his freshman year at Holyoke Community College.

Twisted the ignition key again. More sputtering.

Fire up, you son-of-a-buck!

Finally, the engine took pity on the old woods cop. After a quick J-turn, Murdock drove past the cabin in a cloud of dust with sparks shooting from the exhaust pipe—actually, from the hole in the pipe in front of the rusted muffler. One more back-fire, and the Bronco disappeared, leaving a pall of blue smoke in its trail.

· · ·

MURDOCK BUMPED ALONG A REMOTE DIRT ROAD THAT WAS more of a game trail than an actual thoroughfare. His chunky trail tires kicked out gravel. Clotted chunks of mud had caked inside all four wheel wells before the first freeze. Stayed all dried up in there, now, like gray concrete.

Intermittent static issued from his dash radio. Then, the sultry tones of their female dispatcher offered a welcome respite from the noise that the radio's antiquated squelch could not defeat. Murdock had been warned about his playful flirting. Like he had a shot!

"Unit twenty-one... unit twenty-one... please respond to a shooting complaint near the abandoned hotel at Wolf Hollow."

Shit. Means another hike to the top of that wretched ridge.

He tried not to sound pissed at that silky voice washing over him from his radio's speaker. Or too sarcastic. What was her name, again? "Unit twenty-one received. Thanks a lot!"

"Sorry, Frank. You're the only officer in that district. Complainant states she's heard shots fired there for over a week now."

"Received and en route."

A week-old complaint. Typical.

· · ·

MURDOCK POINTED HIS BRONC UP INTO THE HILLS ON THE winding road toward Wolf Hollow. Clouds of dust swirled behind, but a fair amount of it filled his Bronc, too. Swiss cheese wheel wells'll have that effect.

Coming around a curve too fast, he slammed on his brakes. Even denser dust engulfed him and the Bronc. Almost got jammed up on a fallen tree and half a dozen boulders.

Great. A landslide. Just what I need.

Murdock snatched the microphone from its hook on the dash. "Unit twenty-one on portable at Wolf Hollow."

"Received, twenty-one."

THIS TRAIL'S A CUSS-ED MESS!

Still muttering to himself, he climbed out of the cruiser, surveying the steep incline. Spotted the head of a foot trail he knew led to the abandoned hotel up top.

Murdock chose his steps with care. Didn't need a twisted ankle. Small rocks tumbled around his feet as he walked, rolling down the steep trail behind him, clattering in hardscrabble protest.

Frank stopped for a moment on the incline to do a quick three-sixty. A panoramic view of the countryside from the ridge reminded him why he chose this line of work. Breathtaking. He loved *his* Western Massachusetts mountains.

The wind had picked up. Or more likely, it hadn't, but felt like it up on the ridge. Leaves rustled as they took to the air, skittering across his path.

And there it was—the abandoned hotel. Not much left other than its foundation, a concrete slab, and two camouflaged tents pitched there, all organized like it was a professional operation of some sort. He could guess.

He approached the campsite, now on full alert, and still managed to step right into a still-steaming pile of dog crap.

Shit!

He dragged his soiled boot over a pile of dead leaves that had accumulated up against a rotten log. Still shaking his left boot every other step, Frank continued on into the campsite.

Off to his right hung camo pants drying on a clothesline. There was a wire run for dogs, and the remains of a fire. Just a bed of ashes within an impromptu rock circle.

Murdock soft-stepped up to the rightmost tent that was zippered shut like the other one. He unzipped it, bottom up, for a peek inside. Halfway up, he stooped, pushed aside the flaps, and faced a barking, snarling whirlwind of teeth, fur and blazing eyes, inches away.

He flew butt behind heels onto his ass, stunned by the attack.

Gee-ZEUS!

The big dog choked against his now ribbon-tight chain to get at him from inside that tent.

The hound relented, but continued to snarl in frustration as Murdock got to his feet. As he got to his feet, he noticed drops of blood glistening on the dried leaves near where he had stumbled back. He stooped to run a finger over it.

Still stooping, he sniffed—the drop smelled coppery. Eyeballed it up close. Rubbed it in a circular motion between his right thumb and forefinger. Slippery. Yup. Blood.

After his third three-sixty scan since entering the camp, he followed the intermittent blood trail. He often bragged he could track anything, anywhere, anytime. And he had.

The trail led him to a clearing surrounded by... camouflaged netting? And a game pole constructed of two straight hardwood tree limbs driven into the ground ten feet apart. Someone had strung a rope between the poles eight feet off the ground. Guy ropes outboard of the poles ensured they would support tremendous weight.

He saw four dead bears hanging by their necks. They'd cut off their paws at the wrists and stripped their hides down from their necks to reveal incisions deep into abdominal flesh. Still raw and bloody. And steaming.

What the fuck? A crew of pro poachers!

THE END OF A RIFLE BARREL POKED OUT OF THE BUSHES just twenty yards away, brushing a limb and its dried leaves. The crosshairs of a scope centered on Murdock's back. A finger tightened, and....

MURDOCK SPUN AROUND, REACTING TO A SOUND ANY *normal* sixty-two-year-old pair of ears would have missed. At that moment, a bullet struck Frank three inches above and four inches to the left of his chest's center. He sprawled backwards.

THE POACHER WALKED TOWARD THE FALLEN GAME warden. Leaves crunched beneath his boots in the now deadly silent forest.

Murdock's voice wheezed, "Help. Please."

A raspy laugh echoed in the silence. The poacher's response to Murdock's plea with the rifle pointed at his forehead? A blast that shattered the forest's silence.

The man with the mean eyes kicked the uniformed piece of meat at his feet as he drew in the sweet scent of cordite.

3

DURING AN AFTERNOON DRIVE ALONG THE SHORELINE OF A small mountain lake—Sam Travis forgot if it had a name—he ducked his head to watch a flock of geese fly low before they landed and slid forward onto the lake's mirrored surface. The ripples fanned out behind them.

Travis admired them through his Bronco's open passenger-side window with his left elbow perched out on the driver's side. They now glided on the surface, but as they moved, he knew beneath the surface, they were paddling their asses off. Sort of like an undercover op. Not much was always what it seemed. His radio squawked. Gawd, that Margie had a nice voice.

"Twenty-three is on. Go ahead."

"Unit twenty-one hasn't reported in for two hours. He was on a shooting complaint at Wolf Hollow. Check and see if he's okay?"

"Roger, dispatch. Will do."

The obedient Bronco lurched forward on the dusty road.

Fifteen minutes later, Travis pulled up behind Murdock's cruiser. Got out, sauntered over, and scanned the interior. His friend and partner had locked all the doors. Felt the hood, walked back to his own vehicle.

Travis stretched across the seat from his still-open driver's door. Snatched the microphone by its cord that stretched between the radio on the dash and the middle of the front seat.

As he clutched the mike in his hand, he squeezed, including PTT—the push-to-talk button. "Dispatch from unit twenty-three, I'm on the scene. No sign of Murdock. I'm going in with a portable...."

"Twenty-three, received at 1310 hours."

He tossed the mike back onto the front seat and reached into the back seat to snatch the portable radio. Locked up, and started up the trail.

. . .

TWENTY MINUTES LATER, TRAVIS SPOTTED THE abandoned hotel's concrete slab foundation, or what was left of it. He saw signs of a substantial campsite, but all vestiges of tents, belongings, and what looked like game pole anchors. All gone. He noticed footprints of several men. Less obvious was the blood trail.

He followed it.

After just a few steps, he studied two mounds of earth covered with forest debris. Hair and slivers of pink flesh peeked through the dirt. His skin prickled and his eyes flashed around, now hyper-vigilant.

Drew his revolver and shuffled forward, ensuring that during every moment, he maintained a stable shooting stance. His trusted S&W led the way, held in the low ready position.

A few yards farther out from the vacated camp-site, Travis uncovered the carcass of a black bear. Rolled it over. The animal was missing its head, all four paws and some entrails. Another mound, a second carcass. He flipped it over. Same mutilation. Underneath the second bear's carcass, however, there were the head and shoulders of... Frank Murdock?

Frank's now-sightless eyes were locked open beneath a large-caliber wound that had caved in his forehead. Another entry, upper left torso.

GEE-zus. Dammit, Frank!

Travis scanned the surrounding woods with his gun, eyes wild. Nothing. Birds chirped, wind rustled. He sensed no immediate danger. Then and only then did he collapse to his knees, coughing and gagging.

After his heart had pounded out about two hundred staccato beats, he removed the portable radio from his belt. He just sat there with the radio resting in his lap and his head pounding. Frank was gone. Poor Judy....

After a full minute, in a hoarse whisper... "Dispatch from unit twenty-three—"

4

Twilight now consumed what had been a pleasant afternoon glow. An ambulance's roof lights flashed, reflecting off the dense pines of Wolf Hollow that rose on all sides.

Assorted law enforcement vehicles with clusters of uniformed men stood around taking notes, walking back and forth. Crime scene techs had their yellow tape strung all over the entire area:

POLICE LINE – DO NOT CROSS

It seemed like everyone kept moving, maybe to stave off the "there but for the grace of God" thoughts that invaded their already crappy moods.

One of their own....

Travis thought, *Smells like Christmas out here.*

He sat in the driver's seat of his cruiser, right behind Frank's, with his door open. Gazed at a dirty spot on the windshield in front of him. Out of focus. Their boss, Lieutenant Paul O'Neill, stared down at his pad, pencil in hand, writing nothing. Almost like that was *his* dirty windshield spot.

He said, "If you think of anything else, Sam, call me at headquarters."

Travis said, "Who's gonna to tell Judy?"

"You were his partner. Up to it?"

Travis nodded, still studying that yellow splat on the tempered safety glass in front of him, not daring to look at anything or anyone else just yet. But the sight of the paramedics trudging past with Frank's body bag right outside his open door? How could he not swivel his still-vacant gaze?

They slid Murdock into the ambulance with the ME's permission. The double doors slammed shut five yards away.

Bam, bam.

Travis lurched. Twice. The ambulance wound up and weaved past the other vehicles. Disappeared in a cloud of dust. The techs followed their meticulous protocols photographing everything, searching for, bagging and labeling evidence.

Even though it wasn't yet dark, a faded yellow American Motors Pacer with its high-beams blazing pulled up on the driver's side of Sam's green Bronco, at least as close as the crime scene tape allowed. The newspaper logo was visible on both of the Pacer's doors.

The young woman in her late twenties who turned off the lights and slid out of the Pacer's driver seat looked like an attractive intellectual on safari.

Her oversized glasses, khaki pants tucked into hiking boots, a beige shirt with the sleeves rolled up high on her slender arms—she was a raving beauty who tried to hide it. Didn't work. She shook out her auburn hair that was just too long and thick and wavy to be true.

Everything Kate Miller wore was fresh-pressed, with creases so sharp they looked lethal. She was the Wedgewood Courier's investigative reporter. She hustled up to Travis, still sitting and staring at his appointed spot.

Jerry Benjamin, her photographer, always followed close behind Kate like an eager puppy on a short leash. Today was no exception. For the second time in as many minutes, he shoved his too-cool sunglasses back up his nose. He slammed his passenger-side door. Kate frowned at his insensitivity. Jerry's Nikon camera and various attachments dangled and clinked from his neck.

Now at Travis's side, Kate said, "Sam, I heard it on the scanner."

———

TRAVIS CRAWLED OUT OF HIS BRONCO, HAULING HIS BLANK expression out with him. His holster snagged on the seat cover, then the door with a minor clink. Again. He ignored it. Powered through with a jerk of his hip. Stood there staring at the ground. Just to make sure he wouldn't stumble, not because he still feared looking anyone in the eye. Not really.

"It's Frank."

Kate reached for his hand. He didn't resist. She wrapped her arms around him in slow deliberation. His own just hung at his sides, as if paralyzed. Still, he flinched. No idea why.

Sam Travis stood a good six feet and packed a solid one-ninety. He normally possessed what folks referred to as a *command presence*. Confident, self assured and a military bearing earned from a four-year stint serving his country. Squared-away is what most folks call it. Intimidating but not threatening unless you pushed his buttons. Right now, though, the only presence he felt was emptiness. That would soon be replaced by something else, something dark. Something dangerous.

Kate said, "All I heard was that an officer was down. My God! Was it an accident?"

"The bastards... they must've ambushed him."

"How bad is he, Sam?"

"Dead." Like his eyes.

Like the asshole who killed my partner. He just doesn't know it yet.

Sam felt her shiver. He looked past her. Up-nodded toward his boss a few yards away. "Get a statement from the lieutenant. I gotta go tell Judy."

Without another word, he pulled away, walked back to the Bronco. Its door still hung open. Crawled back in with his right hand on his equipment belt to ensure nothing snagged again. Slammed the creaky door. Needed oil. His radio squawked non-stop.

Kate watched him get in. "When do I see you?"

"I'll call you tonight."

He started the engine and roared off down the dusty road—same direction as the ambulance.

Travis slammed the steering wheel with the heels of both hands as the road jostled him. He winced in pain. Just what he needed.

No, he needed more. A lot more.

5

THE MURDOCK PLACE WAS THE PICTURE OF EARLY EVENING serenity.

The full-length front porch of a rustic farmhouse overlooked an expansive lawn. Travis approached on foot from the road with his chin on his chest. Judy Murdock tended a perennial flower bed near the front steps of the house as daylight grew dim and shadows lengthened.

She wore tight faded jeans with a turtleneck sweater, revealing a youthful figure despite her fifty-plus years. She had gathered a bouquet of day-lilies for a large vase she kept filled with fresh flowers just inside the front door.

Travis knew she loved these beautiful flowers.

Their scent was subtle, and their blooms lasted only for a day or two, but there were so many. She always said they reminded her how sweet and short life could be.

Judy looked up when she sensed motion from the corner of her eye. When she saw Travis, she broke out into a beautiful grin.

This sucks. How am I going to tell her? Just get it done.

ALWAYS LOOKING FOR THE BRIGHT SIDE OF EVERY situation, Judy Murdock beamed at the sight of Sam Travis, Frank's brother officer. As he approached, he looked so exhausted. She'd cheer him up.

"Hi, Sam! Your partner is late again, as usual."

But everything changed as he got closer. Sam started to say something, hesitated, swallowed hard. He tried to straighten his back and shoulders, but they still sagged.

Oh, no!

He said nothing. She could see his jaw muscles working overtime. The poor man just stared, searching for words. Remained silent. Paralyzed.

Her grin faded, her face fell. With widening eyes,

her own jaw dropped, her mouth agape. She knew. But she had to ask.

"Is it Frank?"

Sam reached out with care, took both her hands in both of his. Tears welled up. He drew her in too abruptly, hugged her close. Whispered inches from her left ear, "Frank was killed this afternoon, Jude—"

Judy Murdock pushed him away, propelled by shock and disbelief. Her eyes turned glassy. Her cheeks now stained muddy with tears trailing through an almost invisible sheen of garden dust on her cheeks. She understood the words, but still processed them as if they were in Ancient Greek.

"What? What, what do you mean, killed? What happened? Why?"

She issued a series of sudden intakes of air, not quite ready to allow sobs out loud yet. Her whole body convulsed. This made no sense.

Frank gone? Forever? No. Some mistake!

"I don't have the answers yet, but I will, Jude."

IN THE DAYS TO COME, SHE WOULDN'T REMEMBER SAM picking her up out of her flower bed, or carrying her into the house.

Nor would she remember how she had gotten to the couch in front of the fireplace.

Or Sam taking off her shoes.

Or how the blanket that always lay over the back of the rocker by the wood bin—Frank's favorite chair—ended up covering her.

Had to have been dear Sam. Because there was no Frank. Not anymore. All she'd remember was crying herself into exhaustion. Still, sleep would not come.

Except for the nightmare. The one she'd dreaded their entire married life. That one now cracked her heart wide-open. Every time she closed her eyes. Or opened them and saw Frank's empty rocker.

Yesterday's day-lily blossoms by the front door were long-gone, too.

6

The grounds bristled with freshly painted brick. You could still smell it in the crisp morning's glow. A gilded sign on the lawn near the facility's entrance gate and guardhouse announced this as a military-style installation:

Environmental Police Academy
Framingham, Massachusetts

Some of the old-fashioned buildings on the campus looked even more old-fashioned with pillars and porches. Groups of cadets marched with drill instructors counting cadence.

One of those buildings was a gymnasium. Inside, twenty-five recruits in white t-shirts and long olive drab sweat pants, all emblazoned with the same green and gold EPO logo, sat on the fold-out hardwood bleachers. They rimmed the south side of the basketball court.

The cadets all listened to every word uttered by Captain Larry Jamison, who spoke from a spot on the court in front of the bleachers. He projected a measured, direct, and authoritative voice.

"So, if you remember anything, it's this. According to FBI statistics, EPOs are more likely to be assaulted with dangerous weapons than any other law enforcement group. We work in remote areas, we expect booby-trapped drug fields, commercial poaching rings, satan worshippers—all kinds of crazies with guns. Some are nuts enough to shoot at anyone wearing a badge.

"Worse, our backups are often hours—not minutes—away. In these situations, use your head first. Stall for time. This requires a cool head under intense pressure. Above all, it requires discipline. This is what we will teach you here.

"You, second row, you just volunteered. Over here on the mat."

. . .

JAMISON APPROACHED THE TWENTY-FOOT-SQUARE MAT laid out on the hardwood basketball floor and waited for the large recruit who sheepishly approached him.

"Come at me, son. And don't hold back because I have a few years on you. *Well,* you have your orders... *attack!*"

The kid never knew what hit him. First, Jamison used a series of defensive blocks. A couple of offensive holds later, he threw the kid to the mat. To his credit, the cadet jumped back to his feet, only to experience a series of rapid-fire Wing Chun chain punches.

Once the young man had had enough, Jamison eyed the group who still sat on the bleachers. These were go-getters. He spotted one who broadcast through body language he thought he could do better.

"You. Next."

Wash, rinse, repeat. One after another, each of several cadets returned to the bleachers nursing their badges of foolish courage. It took less than ten minutes to turn a group of youthful skeptics into faces filled with obvious awe and respect.

. . .

A SOLITARY FIGURE STOOD AT THE FAR END OF THE bleachers. Jamison's own training and almost two decades of experience demanded he maintain an acute awareness of his surroundings. That meant he watched entrances, exits, chokepoints, or sought out any potential threats, and how many. The term he'd drum into these cadets was *acute situational awareness.*

The light from the gym door to the west cast the solitary figure in silhouette. Unacceptable. Jamison paced as he delivered his closing remarks to the group of recruits. He worked off adrenaline from the workout. But more importantly, he paced so he could capture a better angle to evaluate that suit who watched his every move and listened to his every word.

The commissioner? Now, what?

COMMISSIONER TOM VERDI'S SQUARE JAW SET HIM APART. So did the lean figure that supported his broad shoulders and a no-nonsense crooked grin of appreciation.

Now, he leaned with impatience against the wall of the gym next to the double-doors that were propped open. He'd spotted Jamison's scanning tactic and moved away from the door's back light to ease his academy commandant's apprehension.

Jamison nodded to the drill instructor in charge of these new cadets as he said, "That's it for today. Sarge, they're all yours. Good luck, men." No female recruits in this class. He'd have to think about that.

The DI nodded back and looked at the men on the bleachers. He hollered, "You heard the man! Hit the showers, ladies!"

Commissioner Verdi wheeled on his heel and marched out the door.

THE TWO MEN WALKED SIDE-BY-SIDE WITHOUT SPEAKING as they headed for Jamison's office. What Commissioner Verdi had to say required privacy.

They approached an ordinary door on the main floor of the academy's administration building. Commissioner Verdi brushed the raised gold letters on the door's frosted window with his fingertips :

Captain L. Jamison,
Academy Commandant

Jamison opened the door and waved his boss

through first. Once he had closed the door behind them, Verdi said, "You still haven't lost it, Jamison."

He comically waved his arms with small abrupt gestures, close to his stomach, accompanied by some farcical head dodges and upper torso moves. Jamison guessed his boss meant to mimic martial arts moves he'd seen in the movies. Or was he trying to be funny?

Every EPO knew the man didn't possess a sense of humor, and was more a Boston politician than a cop.

He said, "Great moves. Bruises from tangling with that big one?" The commissioner grinned.

"I'm glad it doesn't show, anyway." Jamison winced while rubbing his left shoulder.

The secretary had popped her head up from the typewriter as soon as they entered. Ellie chirped, "Good morning, Commissioner."

Verdi's expression signaled she'd just interrupted something important. He smiled and nodded as he brushed by Jamison and slid into his inner office.

Jamison looked at Ellie and shrugged. "He's distracted, Elle. No calls please."

. . .

THE WALL BEHIND JAMISON'S SMALL METAL DESK displayed various plaques, framed certificates, and photos of department dignitaries. That desk almost lacked sufficient vacant space for Jamison to hoist his right hip atop its surface.

The commissioner sat on a small couch that had seen better days. But it was clean. He peered up at his commandant with a serious expression, but said nothing, as if contemplating his next words with great care.

Not a patient man, Jamison said, "So what's up, Commissioner? I know you didn't just stop by to watch another demonstration."

"Okay, yeah. It's about Frank Murdock."

"Good man. Too many unanswered questions about that. You two were classmates, weren't you?"

"Yeah." Verdi took a deep breath and blew it out with some force behind it, inflating both his sculpted cheeks for a couple of beats before he spoke again. Jamison could hear the sorrow. "I'm initiating our own investigation into his murder. Separate from the DA's."

"Why? And what's that got to do with me, boss?

"I want you to head it up. "

The silence jangled both their nerves. Then....

"I don't think so, Commissioner. You know about Maggie and me. I bid on this job to stop the divorce proceedings. Twenty years of weekends, holidays and nights.... Respectfully, forget it. Find someone else."

"Captain Jamison, I want you. Murdock was more than one of my officers and a classmate. I'm godfather to his son, for chrissakes. He was my closest friend on the job. This is personal. Besides, you're still the best investigator this department's got. Come on, Larry...."

At that moment, Verdi didn't look like his boss. Looked more like a puppy dog whose paw had just been stomped on. Jamison walked to the wall and focused on a photo of him and Maggie.

He pointed at the photo. "Great. Just great. It's the last nail in that coffin and you're helping me drive it in."

Verdi said nothing. He waited. The likable son-of-a-bitch didn't even look like he felt guilty asking, just hurt. To the quick.

The silence stretched to ten seconds, twenty, thirty....

Jamison wheeled on his heels to glare at his boss. His face flushed. Blood pounded in his temples. His jaw muscles got a workout, too.

"This damn job's always been my mistress. Maggie never understood that. Probably my fault, anyway. Okay. If it gets dirty, I want your word—*in*

GK JURRENS

writing—that you authorized this little operation. Otherwise, no deal."

After just one more shaky breath, Verdi said without hesitation, "Give me some paper and a damn pen."

JAMISON AND HIS BOSS STROLLED OUT ONTO THE quadrangle between the academy's administration building and the exercise grounds. En route, they passed cadets and their K-9 units working their highly trained tracking dogs. The two men shook hands as they approached the VIP parking lot.

ALONE, CAPTAIN LARRY JAMISON OBSERVED HIS OWN FEET marching toward his six-year-old Dodge Diplomat... and toward the likely end of his marriage. Got in and slammed his door harder than he intended.

7

Muddy boots pounded over an even muddier trail. But the stuff had grown semi-stiff with the chilly afternoon temps.

Hounds on the trail galloped through the shallow, gurgling water with abandon. Two young bucks bounded through the trees like their tails were on fire. They only knew mortal danger chased them. They had no idea they weren't targets—just in the wrong place at the right time.

A black bear scrambled up an ancient red oak. The crazed hounds circled the tree. Their yelping echoed through the nearby ravines. Leaping and foaming at the mouth, the dogs were relentless. The poacher preferred hunting with a rifle, but he couldn't afford the attention in this wildlife sanctuary. Using his bow and arrow was the right choice. He aimed and....

Whoosh!

Captain Larry Jamison took silly pride in the precision operation of his remote garage door opener. He'd ensure the overhead door was high enough for his hood to pass underneath in the nick of time.

The rise of the windshield and the car's roof would miss the door by less than an inch on the rest of the door's journey upward as his Dodge rolled in. He smiled every time it actually worked.

Once inside, he slid out of the driver's seat and entered through the garage's service door into the kitchen.

"Maggie, I'm home!"

The liquor cabinet around the corner in the living room from the short hallway that led to the garage door he'd just entered practically opened itself. Her muffled voice came from the bedroom at the end of the hall now to his right.

"In here!"

His drink was already half gone by the time he

reached the spare bedroom at the rear of the four-bedroom rambler. She stood with her back to him at the ironing board set up in the corner near the electrical outlet.

Maggie maneuvered the iron's cord around one of his uniform shirts, the steam burning in the spray starch with which she'd just soaked his collar and sleeves. He nodded toward the shirt and smiled. Said, "Thanks."

"Yeah, well, these things don't iron themselves. And if they did, you wouldn't like it. They wouldn't stand at attention for you and salute." To emphasize her point, she snapped the collar by launching her index finger off her thumb. The result? A satisfying *thwack*.

"Did that stain come out?"

"Yup. You're home early, and you're starting early, too. She flipped a half-assed nod over her left shoulder toward the already-evaporated double in his hand."

"Babe, I'd like to talk to you about something."

He could tell that wasn't the smoothest way to start this out. She rolled her eyes before closing them and wagging her head side to side as her chin sunk to her chest. Apparently, she could iron without looking. She took a breath and sighed. "So, talk. I'm listening."

"Commissioner Verdi has asked me to investigate Frank's murder."

She spun around with her eyes now flashing and the iron clenched in her fist in front of her. "And of course you said you would. Like you always do. You promised me, Larry. You gave me *your word!*"

"I know. Just temporary." As he said the words, they even sounded lame to him.

"For God's sake, Larry, why you? Do I even *look* that stupid? The Murdock case will consume you!"

"Maggie, I'm not giving up my academy job."

"No? How about your *life?* And me?" She waited. He gathered his thoughts. This was not going well. As expected.

SHE WASN'T DONE. "YOU PUT ME THROUGH HELL DURING your last undercover assignment. After you got shot, I watched you lying there in that hospital bed, not knowing...."

For no good reason, his temper flared. "This isn't just another investigation, Maggie. This was a cold-blooded murder of one of our best officers. I promise I'll be more careful." He lowered himself onto the edge of the bed. Patted the space next to him.

She set the iron down so hard on the board that it almost collapsed. She jerked the cord from the wall and tossed it to the floor. Her lips quivered around the genesis of an angry snarl as her eyes misted over.

"Bullshit. You haven't learned a thing. You've made your choice. Now I'm making mine."

With that, she turned, hesitated for a beat as if reconsidering, then marched out the bedroom door. Slammed it shut so hard, the dust on top of the door drifted down into the room like an exclamation point. Or a final curtain slowly descending over yet another tale of heroic dedication... and epic tragedy.

Jamison slouched on the bed, his head down, staring at his empty glass.

8

Decisions produce consequences, don't they?

Still lying in bed the next morning, in the dark—alone—Jamison rubbed the crud from his eyes so he could see the phone's dial well enough to reach out and touch someone. Anyone.

He needed help. Who better than a fellow officer? One that didn't know him all that well. Yet.

"Travis, this is Captain Jamison." He sucked in some badly needed oxygen. "I need to talk to you today.

It's important. Can you meet me at that diner in the center of town? Waddaya call it... the Tivoli? The Rivoli?"

Shit.

"Right. The Beverly."

"Captain, no offense, man, you sound like crap. Hey, you got hip boots, don'tcha?"

"What? Hip boots? Yeah, I got 'em."

"Bring 'em, boss."

"See you in an hour."

Wedgewood, Massachusetts
Beverly's Diner

BEVERLY'S WAS THE PLACE TO GET GOOD FOOD, STRONG coffee, and lots of street gossip. Jamison scanned the joint's hazy interior. Busy servers scurried to booths in their respective sections with loaded trays. Some balanced them overhead to get through pinch points.

He spotted Travis hunched over a steaming mug in a window booth with the mini-juke on the wall below the window turned down low. As Jamison got close, he recognized the song: *Livin' on a Prayer* by

Bon Jovi. Travis nodded his head to the beat. Might've even been lip-syncing.

The whole place reeked of coffee and corned beef hash. Almost covered up the stank of stale smoke from a couple of duffers puffing away at the counter—the smoking section, closer to the greasy ventilation fan on the side wall.

Travis sat alone. Nodded when he spotted his boss's boss by the door near the cash register. Jamison slid in across from his younger EPO. Was just as good as Murdock, maybe better. A few years less experience, was all.

Jamison winced at the lop-sided grin that slowly formed on his subordinate's stubbled face, the kind that said he was staring at one hung-over big-shot now slouched across from him.

Travis whispered so as not to aggravate the obvious head throb he was looking at. "What brings you back into the pucker brush, Captain? Or should I say *Commandant?*"

He looked at the youthful smart-ass sitting across from him. "How about cutting me some slack? Trouble at home, okay?"

"Oh, boy. Sorry." The grin disappeared. Almost.

"Look, Sam, I've been assigned by the commish to lead an investigation into Murdock's death."

TRAVIS SAT BACK, INTRIGUED. THEIR SERVER SWUNG BY. They both ordered the blue plate special. She nodded, looked them both in the eye, didn't say a word, and left. She knew when to be cordial, and when to keep her trap shut. Not her first goat rodeo. Travis liked her for that.

Jamison leaned forward. He did the same. Under his breath, Jamison said, "The commissioner wants to make sure that everything gets looked at. Anyway, you and Murdock were tight. Was he working on anything specific on his own?"

"Nothing special that I know of." But Jamison saw there was something.

"What about this bear stuff?"

"You mean the missing paws and heads? Well, I vaguely remember reading about a case in the southeast a few years back. They were taking the parts and selling them for pretty good money."

"Is there enough money in it to be a motive for murder?"

"Beats me. But I did find him with a couple of carcasses."

"Any idea where we can find out what they get and where the stuff goes?"

"I'll check around for you." He knew somebody who was already looking at this stuff. He'd ask Kate.

"Sam, the Feds might have some information on it. I'll call them."

With startling enthusiasm, Travis said, "Damn right. We've gotta get moving on this."

"We?"

"Yeah, boss. He was my partner, for chrissakes. I *need* to be a part of this. Do you have a problem with *we*?"

Jamison took the measure of this man.

Do I really want him in? Is he stable enough? Perhaps too personally involved? Was Frank's partner....

Questions raced through his mind. Then Jamison relented.

"Okay. For now, it's we. Because I've got to start somewhere. You'll do as you're told. No vigilante moves. And anything we do is confidential. Understood?"

Travis didn't hesitate. He said, "Fair enough. You've got a good reputation from back when you were in the field, Jamison, and we'll do it your way, unless you fuck up. And if you do, you'll hear about it from me, loud and clear."

A smirk creased Jamison's face as their server *stomped* up so as not to surprise them—so they could stop talking before she'd overhear. She was a real pro, alright, and knew the tippers better'n they know themselves. Carried a truck-sized tray of steaming food practically dripping grease on them. Both men smiled big, for more than one reason.

They ate like wolves. After destroying their blue plates, both semi-catatonic men shuffled out of Beverly's—Travis to his Bronco and Jamison to his Dodge parked next to it.

Travis said, "Did you bring your boots?"

"They're in the trunk. What do I need them for?"

"There's a guy shooting ducks over the limit on a marsh near Cranberry Lake. I've been trying to nail this guy for the last two seasons. Figured on you coming, sort of like a good luck charm... Captain... sir.

Jamison grunted and opened his trunk while Travis stood there, grinning—the first real sign of an impending friendship.

9

THE PLOP-SWISH OF CRANBERRY LAKE'S CRYSTAL WATER lapping against a dense thicket of autumn-bristled marsh weeds made its own rather sweet music.

A contented mallard duck honked in the early morning hush. He couldn't help but display his iridescent green feathers in contrast to his earth-tone finery.

The indignant mallard navigated with a natural serenity through the reeds that were dry on top and soggy down below. Made this scene worthy of a Robert Bateman wildlife painting. Its benign title might be *A Duck in Autumn*. The artist would let the colors and the composition in magnificent splendor speak for themselves.

Crisp rustling orchestrated by a pleasant breeze made it clear the orange and red and gold leaves would soon find their way to the forest floor.

Tires crunched over gravel just on the far side of the lake's shoreline thickets. Jamison and Travis opened their doors, slid out of Sam's olive-drab Bronco, and softly closed their doors. They trudged their way toward the marsh, now both in hip boots, panting and sweating in no time.

A Great Blue Heron burst into flight nearby, startling them. It swept over the marsh as it glided ever higher on the breeze. Travis smiled over at Jamison but said nothing. Silence once again reigned.

Then, off in the distance, they heard, *BOOM. BOOM.*

The officers crouched low, frozen in their tracks.

Travis pointed, saying nothing. They both followed the smooth flight of a Canada goose low in the sky until it started tumbling downward. Another loud report echoed down the small lake.

Travis whispered, "Twelve-gauge."

Jamison nodded.

The goose plopped into the water. Ripples radiated.

Travis signaled Jamison. He whispered, "Flank him on the left. I'll stay right. We'll cut him off."

Jamison nodded and smirked, enjoying this. "Too bad he didn't wait for the season to open."

Travis headed out across the marsh in a crouch. Might have been unnecessary since the thicket stood a good foot above his head. Jamison slogged along the edge of the thicket, each moving toward the violator from different directions.

Jamison looked down and in front of him in disgust. A struggling, wounded duck was trapped between clumps of duck weed. Others lay dead, their heads underwater.

That's when he spotted the blind that concealed a solitary hunter. Nearby, the poacher had scattered an array of a dozen decoys in front of the blind. Jamison approached from behind.

The grizzled guy held his twelve-gauge pump-action high, aiming for another flight of incoming ducks.

MEANWHILE, DEEPER IN THE MARSHY THICKET, TRAVIS WAS in trouble. He was sinking in the marsh's gooey bottom a little at a time. Water now poured over the top of his boots. The cold water hit him like a high-voltage shock.

Shit!

The noise of his struggle caught the violator's attention. Travis felt helpless, but he projected more authority in his voice than his vulnerable predicament should have allowed.

"State Environmental Police. Unload your weapon and stand by for inspection."

Fuck!

The bottom's sticky mud sucked at the boots of his waders. Trying to backtrack, one boot came free, the other did not. He fell forward into the muck.

Both the hunter and Jamison appeared amused by this shit show. They both stood in confused amazement. The hunter still had not spotted Jamison behind him.

DARK BROWN MUD NOW SPATTERED TRAVIS'S FACE. HIS eyes shot sparks. He clung to his new mantra: "Fuck!"

The hunter cupped his hands and shouted, "I wouldn't go that way if I were you, Officer."

Travis ignored him. Still knee deep and then some, he continued slogging forward, one agonizing step after the other, until he was within ten feet of the hunter.

His breathing now labored, Travis shivered from

the icy water that had filled his boots. The mud already drying on his face caused his skin to crinkle and shrink. His voice now filled with disdain, accompanied by a sneer that told the violator how disgusted he was, he said, "You're under arrest. You—"

The bottom fell away. The last thing both the hunter and Jamison saw were eyes the size of dinner plates just before Travis disappeared. Only his EPO ball cap marked the spot. And a few slurpy ripples. Unlike Travis, his hat refused to sink.

A few heartbeats later, bubbles started popping at the bullseye. And an instant after that, Travis broke through the surface like a Poseidon missile. He spewed water intermixed with an impressive explosion of gagging and coughing. Weeds hung on one shoulder, and a brown slurry bubbled from one nostril.

Once he'd gathered his wits, Travis looked up at Jamison, already holding the hunter by his left arm. Jamison and the hunter looked at each other.

The hunter said, "Deep hole, huh?"

"Fuck you, mister."

WITH THE HUNTER SECURED IN THE BACK SEAT OF THE Bronco, Travis sat on a dead log to pull off his waders. He up-ended them. Water poured out. Then dribbled out stringy weeds and oozing mud. Smelled like duck shit.

And shame.

Jamison couldn't resist. "God, you're good. I've never seen an arrest quite like that one."

"Sir, with all due respect, fuck you very much."

THE RADIO SQUAWKED, "UNIT TWENTY-THREE, UNIT twenty-three from dispatch."

Still dripping duck-dung soup, Travis reached inside to grab the mike. He glanced over at Jamison. "Looks like I won't get to change yet." Into the mike he said, "Unit twenty-three is on. Go ahead."

"Please respond to an illegal hunting complaint in the state forest off Creamery Road where the brook intersects. Complainants will meet you there. They'll be driving a brown pickup."

"Received. As soon as we drop off our guest at the State Police lock-up, we're en route."

10

IT WAS BEAUTIFUL OUT HERE. THE COLORS IN THE LOW meadow alongside Creamery Road had not yet blossomed into their autumnal splendor.

Rocks the size of houses glistened with wet moss. The torrent of water cascading over them exploded with a bouquet of miniature rainbows in the mist. A kingfisher took to flight with a small baitfish in its bill. They saw all this as they rolled alongside the creek that ran parallel to the road for a stretch.

The green Bronco stopped on a small wooden bridge that spanned Rocky Creek where it intersected the road. Two hikers stood by a brand-spanking tricked-out brown Subaru BRAT and flagged the two officers down.

Travis looked at his boss and whispered, "Pickup, my ass. That's a yuppie truckette. You know what BRAT stands for? *'Bi-drive Recreational All-terrain Transporter.'* Read that in Popular Mechanics. Was so funny, I just had to memorize it."

Jamison whispered back, "You're shitting me."

"I shit you not, boss."

Jamison and Travis walked up to the couple. Jamison said, "What's up, folks?"

The twenty-something man with a short pony tail that poked out the bottom of a wool watch cap said, "Two does ran by us near the hemlock stand a quarter mile in while we were picking mushrooms. We then heard three quick shots and voices right after. Came out and called you right away."

The weedy girl with him nodded with energy. She blew out an explosive breath and shook her head from side to side—the universal language of disgust. She looked about fifteen, but she wore a wedding band. So did Pony Tail. Plus, their clothes were both trendy and expensive. So was the BRAT. Two healthy incomes, for sure. Travis thought, *Good for them.*

He said to nobody in particular, "Seems like the season for poaching never closes." He mimicked the girl's expression. "Okay, folks, give my partner here the exact location again while I get my map."

Sam tugged at his wet crotch and rolled his eyes while shaking his head as an unspoken apology for digging south of the border while in mixed company. He hiked back to his Bronco while the couple chatted with Jamison.

11

ARMED WITH THE LOCATION, THE TWO WARDENS LEFT THE yuppie hikers after thanking them and tromped off into the woods.

Travis squished along in his still-soaked shoes. He'd had to tighten his laces since wet leather stretches. Also, the onset of what was sure to be crotch rot distracted him as he tugged at his boxers through his uniform trousers. He kept repeating to himself, *This sucks. This really sucks. I love my job. I really do love my job. Otherwise....*

Jamison spotted the silent drama unfolding. He was getting tired of rolling his eyes, and said so.

They stared at the trail, searching for tracks or any evidence of the deer or poachers. Jamison bent down on a hunch. Found some turned over leaves. And a splotch of blood the size of a silver dollar on a rock.

"Travis, take a look." He nodded down toward the rock. The younger man said, "Looks like our boys. Let's not stick too close together. I'll stay on their trail and you hang off to one side and behind."

"I've been doing this a lot longer than you, sonny." Jamison puckered one cheek, cocked his head and glanced at Travis slantwise.

"Okay, pops," Travis whispered, nodding and glancing up ahead with a bob of his head. "Movement."

Travis kept walking. Jamison hung back. Fifty yards later, the woods grew more silent than was reasonable. The faint sound of boots crunching over dry leaves ahead caused Travis to freeze in his tracks near a rotted stump.

On its far side, he spotted a freshly killed doe. A young one. There was that crunching sound again. He started moving toward what had to be the poacher.

JAMISON WATCHED TRAVIS UP THE TRAIL, NEGOTIATING each step with care. Stealth mode. Had to smile. He wasn't all that quiet, but the forest was... now. Alarmed, Jamison crouched and waited as Travis stopped to examine something on the far side of a downed tree. A big one. Then he moved forward. With purpose. Travis was tracking.

Then Jamison saw him—the poacher. Or one of them, since Travis seemed to be tracking someone—or something—else. A camouflaged man with a rifle crept out of the brush and tracked Travis.

Still concealed, Jamison moved like an old cat to get behind and closer to this bastard—close enough to *smell* the ripe son-of-a-bitch.

From behind a boulder and a cluster of young birches, he watched as the guy raised his rifle to his shoulder. Pointed it at his partner's back, who was still hiking away. Yup, Travis was tracking someone else. That meant at least two of them to contend with. Consistent with the voices the yuppies overheard. Jamison glanced back at his own flank, but there was nobody back there. As far as he could tell, anyway.

The poacher's cheek now pressed to the stock, he took careful aim at Travis. Now he and this asshole shared the same enormous boulder. He reached around from behind and grabbed the muzzle of the gun. Gave a mighty jerk, and the rifle came free. Jamison already had his pistol pointed at the surprised deer poacher's chest.

Jamison said, "Hi. Environmental Police. I'll be arresting you today."

Louder, "Like hell you are."

As the poacher took a wild swing at Jamison. He blocked it with the rifle. The guy winced as a bloody welt raised on the knuckles of his right hand. Another swing. Same action, same result.

Jamison lectured the idiot. "The definition of doing the same thing and expecting a different result? Insanity, my friend."

"What can you do without a gun, hero?"

Jamison shrugged, holstered his revolver, set the poacher's rifle on the forest floor after snicking on its safety. The oaf tried to kick Jamison's head while he was bent over.

Was that supposed to be a martial arts move?

Jamison grabbed the guy's boot, twisted, and drove an elbow up into the now-off-balance poacher's nose. Blood gushed in the same instant he heard the soft crunch of ligaments snapping. Now on the ground and pacified, Jamison stooped down to cuff his hands around a stout sapling that stood tall by this dipshit's shoulder.

Jamison looked at this younger man still wiping blood and snot on the sleeve of his free arm and said, "Not bad for an old hero, eh, sonny? Didn't your daddy teach you not to start something you can't finish?" He followed the remark with a legendary smirk of self-satisfaction.

The element of surprise helped.

FURTHER UP THE TRAIL, TRAVIS CLOSED ON THE SECOND poacher, who was dragging another deer. With his chest heaving from the effort, sweat dripped from his nose despite the chilly temps. Travis could see the poacher's breath fifteen feet away. He stole up behind him with his pistol drawn and said, "Give it up."

Breathing even harder, sweat poured off the man. Eyes darting, a picture of panic, he held his rifle in his right hand while refusing to let go of the dead deer. The guy froze with indecision.

Now less than an arms-length away, Travis said with an eerie calm, "Put the gun down." Nothing. "Put the gun down, now." He punctuated his words with a jab in the poacher's back with the business end of his three-five-seven.

The panicked hunter slowly set the rifle down,

now shaking. But he still hung onto the deer's right rear leg. He turned to face Travis. He was older, maybe married, with a good job. Maybe he owned a home, maybe he had no criminal record of any kind. Just a guy who made a bad decision.

Jamison approached them, watching the drama unfold. Travis spotted Jamison and held up his non-gun hand toward his boss. "I got this."

With Travis distracted, the hunter dropped the dead deer's leg, reached down, and picked up his rifle. For an older guy, he was scary fast. By the time Travis swiveled his head back, the old guy had his rifle pointed at Travis's chest.

Shit!

Panicked, the hunter's eyes darted from officer to officer.

Travis kept his pistol trained on the guy's chest, but tamped down with his left palm and said, "Easy, man. This is crazy. You've killed two deer. That's all. Don't make it worse.'

With this turn of events, Jamison drew his holstered revolver with slow deliberation. Travis turned and saw what the poacher saw.

Travis said, "It's ok, Larry."

The poacher *snicked* off his rifle's safety.

"Think, pal. You don't need this kind of trouble."

The hunter's 's finger tightened on his trigger.

"Put it down. No one will get hurt. Put it down."

In the silence, Travis felt an icy trickle of sweat roll down his back inside his shirt and jacket. Thinking hard, he looked into the poacher's flashing eyes that started misting over and said, "I'm just going to put my gun back into my holster. Okay?"

He felt the barrel of his revolver sliding into leather.

"See? No one will get hurt."

Time stopped. It was *so* quiet.

"It's okay."

Travis reached out haltingly with his right hand, moved his left hand closer to the end of the rifle's barrel, still pointed at his gut. Gripped the barrel, pulled with care so as not to trip that damn trigger.

The poacher shook as he released his grip on the rifle's stock. Travis watched as his finger eased on out of the trigger guard.

The man fell to his knees and released a series of wracking sobs.

Travis realized he hadn't been breathing. Not really. He exhaled. Unloaded the rifle and laid it on the ground since loaded rifles leaned against a tree have been known to go off if they fall.

THEN JAMISON BREATHED, TOO.

Travis pivoted and whacked the poacher on the back of his head with his open palm and said, "You crazy bastard! Over a couple a fuckin' deer?"

Then, as he spun him around to cuff him, in a shaky voice, Travis said, "You're under arrest, asshole."

12

WEDNESDAY,

October 5th

Wedgewood, Massachusetts

TRAVIS MISSED HER. HE'D FIX THAT STRAIGHTAWAY.

The Bronco found a parking space on the diagonal half a block away. That's how everybody parked on Main—diagonally to the curb. There were no lines on the street, but it worked fine. Small town.

He never locked his doors in town—only out in the woods. Approached the front door of the Wedgewood Courier's red brick, two-story building. He looked up at the six-foot-high raised letters above the door. They lit up after dark, didn't they? He couldn't remember. Not important. He was never here at night.

Inside, past a small art deco reception area, a half-dozen reporters chattered with editors at their desks. Some pounded away at computers or checked files in drawers at the long line of filing cabinets on the wall to his left.

A wall—half glass up top, half sheet rock on the bottom—separated a row of offices straight ahead toward the back, behind the busy bullpen where everyone except management and the senior editor worked.

This place was a beehive of activity in a windowless room with bright fluorescents. Stunk of newsprint and caged energy. Minimum outside distraction. Travis instantly felt trapped. Not that he was claustrophobic. Much. He preferred the great outdoors.

Who doesn't? And jeez, this noise!

Kate Miller stood at a five-drawer file cabinet off to his left, flipping through manilla folders captured in dark green hanging folders. She pulled out a fistful and hustled back to her desk. He entered the newsroom. She lit up when she spotted him.

It surprised nobody as he sauntered over to her desk to sneak a quick peck on her cheek. Pulled up a chair and sat down with his elbows on his knees. Had they been just casual acquaintances—they weren't—he'd be invading her personal space.

Travis said, "Find anything we could use?"

"Hello to you, too. I might have. It was in the environmental and not the police files. Here. How's Judy?" She slid a folder to her left on her cluttered desktop, close to his left elbow.

"Not good, but she's strong. She and Frank...." He didn't want to talk about that right now.

As Travis abruptly grabbed the folder—not much in it—he flipped it open, started reading a clipped article. The headline and photo represented its contents: *The Killing Game: Bears, Sex, and Folk Medicine.*

In the center of the article's cover page was a picture of a bear's severed head, along with its paws and gall bladder, sealed in a plastic bag.

"Aphrodisiacs.... Jeez, should we try some of this stuff?"

"Get serious, Sam."

SHE KNEW HE WAS KIDDING. STILL....

He said, "I'm working with Captain Larry Jamison. He's the academy commandant. The commissioner yanked him away to head up the Murdock case."

Kate scrunched her nose, which also puckered her forehead. "So, how are you involved? Are you suggesting that Frank's murder and this are related?" She sideways nodded down toward the open file in his hands.

Travis wrinkled his own forehead, cocked his head toward his right shoulder, tossed her a one-shoulder shrug. "Dunno. Maybe. Can I take this? I wanna show it to Larry. By the way, if you can't reach me, here's Jamison's card with his number."

"Okay, sure. That copy's for you." She nodded toward the folder.

Kate slid Jamison's card into her wallet on the desk. Next to a coffee mug, in front of a can of pencils beside her computer, and a forest of dead trees: no less than eight teetering piles of paper.

She tossed her wallet, which was more like a clutch purse about the size and profile of a misshapen soccer ball. She said without looking at Sam, "So, what's your role in this investigation?" He could hear just the slightest quiver in her voice. Her eyes looked down at nothing, but she seemed to see something he couldn't. Yet.

Another one-shoulder shrug. "Just doing some prelim work for Jamison, is all."

"Yeah, right."

With a dismissive wave, he said, "Are we on for tonight?"

"I'd love to, Sam, but I need to do a follow-up story on this bear business."

"Okay. Then how about dinner with Brian and me tomorrow night?"

She hesitated, swiveled her chair to read his eyes with new concern in hers. "Gee, Sam, I don't know. Won't he be uncomfortable?"

"Look, Liz died two years ago. We'll always love and miss her, but I'm tired of hiding you from Brian. Come to the house tomorrow. I'll fix a nice meal and we'll talk. It's time for him to know about us, even though he still misses his mom. For God's sake, Kate, we love each other."

She leaned back in her chair and smiled. Her dimples appeared. Made him weak in the stomach, but strong-like-bull farther south.

"Well, hooray for us."

13

OUT OF BED THE NEXT MORNING, BARELY, JAMISON COULD almost ignore the stench of rancid Chinese takeout. Last night's desiccated egg fu yung had long since dried onto the dinner plate in the sink, and the gelatinized gravy carved weird curly-cues around the edge of its plastic take-out container still on the countertop. Put him right off Chinese omelets. Maybe forever. Maybe not. The lid had landed on the floor. He hadn't bothered to pick it up. Wasn't sure why. He was a fastidious guy. Used to be, anyway.

Goddammit!

Maggie... he missed her. Wondered if she missed him. Brought a lump to his throat.

What the hell am I doing?

A jumble of glasses, newspapers, and silverware cluttered most of every horizontal surface in the kitchen and dining room.

His hapless gaze scanned the chaos.

How'd this happen so fast?

And evidence of no female supervision didn't stop there. As he passed from the kitchen to the living room, he winced as he glanced down the hall. The open bathroom door revealed more than one pile of towels and clothing on the tiled floor.

He slumped into the master bedroom, looked at his nightstand. The digital alarm clock reminded him again he'd overslept by half an hour. Again. The framed photo of him and Maggie next to his empty rocks glass reminded him he'd put the job first. Again.

It was 5:30. The damn sun was already up. The phone rang. Startled out of even more self-pity, Jamison reached over and crammed the receiver against his left ear. He wondered whether the painful *whack* against his skull right behind his wife-deaf right ear was intentional. He deserved it, didn't he?

"What?"

Half an hour earlier, Travis had slipped into his favorite white tank top, boxer shorts, and shower clogs. Then a brain fart struck him like a bolt of high-amperage inspiration.

He paced the floor with the spiraled and knotted phone cord trailing behind. Looked like it would stretch maybe another three feet, or a little more. Sipped his coffee—finally the right color and temp —while he waited for Jamison to answer.

Travis heard Larry bark, wondering what *that* was all about. He'd ask him later. For now, he just said, "Larry, I just remembered. There's this guy named Taggart. He's a mountain man, a recluse, a grizzly old buck."

"Jesus, Sam—"

"Yeah, yeah, I know what time it is. Larry, this guy and Murdock had a thing for a few years. This character has fractured every game law in the book. But Murdock liked the ol' goat. My hunch is that he might fill us in on anything going on in those hills."

"Yeah, alright. Sounds like we should talk to this old outlaw."

"Great. If he'll talk to *us*. He lives in a tar-paper shack somewhere on October Mountain. I'll come get you. Oh, one other thing. Bring your hiking boots."

14

THE NORTHERN GOSHAWK IS KNOWN FOR HIGH-SPEED stealth attacks from out of the sun. Two soared overhead on the ridge line's mid-morning thermal updrafts, announcing their presence with piercing screeches, outraged at the pair of human intruders below.

Steep hemlock stands with the sun glistening through their half-bare branches punctuated the open fields around them.

Ribbons of water cascaded over huge rocks.

A Blue Jay scolded someone or something with

her raucous rebuke from the top branch of an ancient oak.

A ponderous black bear lumbered away, his silvery coat rippled over his fatty pre-winter torso as he disappeared into the shadows.

Life marched on.

THE OLD GREEN BRONCO GROUND ALONG THE WILDERNESS road riddled with potholes you could lose a Volkswagen in. They ran over rotting branches and other forest debris that had succumbed to gravity.

On a not-so-gentle incline where Travis skidded to a stop, Jamison crawled out to drag a fallen limb out of the way. Travis leaned out the driver's side window and sniggered, "Boy, glad I brought you along! Do you do windows too?"

Jamison turned and faked a groan as he tossed the hefty limb aside with little effort. He sauntered back and slung himself into the passenger seat, where the door still stood open.

He winced at the protest of screeching hinges as he slammed the door a little too hard. Didn't take. Took a second try. "Your door could use some Three-in-One, partner."

"Who has time for oil?" Travis grinned. His boss's boss chuckled.

They continued their ascent up the mountain.

Jamison talked as they bounced. His voice bounced, too. "Well, what kind of relationship did Murdock have with this old bark pirate?"

Travis said, "As Frank told it, they loved to play tricks on each other. Sorta cat and mouse. He had to bust Taggart a couple a times, though. Wasn't easy. Frank liked the ol' geezer a lot. Said he was a good shit, just too untamed for game laws. But he only hunted for food. Clamping cuffs on him had to be rough. He trusted ol' Silas Taggart."

Travis made small talk. He and Jamison didn't have that much in common on a personal level. "Speaking of Frank and his tricks, I remember when I was a rookie. He and I were working this case together. Jackers wounded a doe, and we were tracking it. Frank was already a legend.

"He picked something up from the ground, put it to his nose, sniffed it, then put it in his mouth. It was deer shit. Frank turns to me and says, 'she ain't hurt bad. She's only ten minutes ahead of us, Sammy.' He says, 'you can't know a wounded animal until you taste 'em.'

"So I figured, he's a legend, he knows. Naturally, I bent down and swallowed a whole fuckin' handful.

Well, sir, I threw up all over that mountain. I found out at a Christmas party a year later he swapped *Raisinets* for the deer shit—you know, those chocolate covered raisins."

Jamison broke into a wide grin as Travis stopped the truck. They crawled out, rolled up the windows, and locked the doors.

As they moved up the steep trail toward the ridge on foot, Jamison followed Travis. Both breathed hard after a few dozen yards. A bright blue sky met them at the summit. They stopped, huffing hard, and both took a knee. Travis plucked a compass from his jacket pocket. Took a bearing.

He said, "Over there. Gotta be Taggart's shack."

If autumn hadn't already harvested its fair share of leaves, they'd have missed it. Through the trees ahead and to their left, deep in the shadows of a thick copse of oaks, Travis pointed toward a small one-windowed tar-papered structure sagging under its own weight.

As they got closer, they saw two rusted fifty-gallon drums that were once bright yellow leaning against the shack's east wall on lumpy ground and a thick bed of dried pine needles.

They spotted something that seeped through one of the barrel walls where rust had reduced its thickness to paper-thin. If that was a petroleum product, it was a firebomb waiting to be ignited.

Someone, probably Taggart, had stacked at least two cords of firewood close by. He had also littered empty paper milk cartons in and around garbage and metal scraps of all kinds. Some accumulated into piles. A catastrophe on a short fuse awaited.

They approached the shack with caution. Jamison hung two paces back with the heel of his right hand resting on the butt of his holstered revolver. Travis peered through the filthy windowpane on the front wall. Said, "He's not here, far as I can tell."

Jamison relaxed half a notch. He puckered one cheek and snorted. "Where's the Jacuzzi?"

Travis swung the door open. Its hinges screeched. After entering, they shuffled around in near darkness. A pot-bellied stove was cold. They could see daylight around the edge of its pipe where it ascended through the sagging ceiling. Inside the stove's open door, embers had devolved into amorphous white ash. One rickety chair propped up a table with a missing leg. The place was barren except for several unlit candles burned down almost to their wicks' ends and pooled onto the scarred tabletop.

Jamison scrunched up his nose and winced. "What a stench!"

They both froze at the unmistakable sound behind them of a round being racked into the chamber of a venerable .30-.30 lever-action rifle. Turning around slowly—alarmed and surprised—they faced a disheveled man with sunken eyes and a tobacco-stained white beard.

Jamison tamped both palms downward in front of him as he spoke. "Mr. Taggart?"

"You tryin' to steal my shit, huh?

Travis took his turn. "Easy, ol' fella. We just wanna talk to you about your friend."

"Ain't got no friends. Don't need none, neither. I don't like people and 'specially don't like 'em on my land, flashin' badges 'n sidearms." He held that rifle at waist level, but at six feet, aiming was optional.

It was Jamison's turn. "Mr. Taggart, it's our friend, Frank Murdock."

"Who?"

Travis said, "Murdock, you know, the game warden?"

"Ain't here 'n I ain't seen 'im."

"Mr. Taggart, he's dead. Murdered."

The emaciated old man held the scarred 30-30 Winchester steady, still aimed in their general direction. But Taggart's resolve weakened. His face registered disbelief, then shock. Lowered the rifle to his side after easing the hammer home. Gripped it by the barrel.

Travis continued. "Mr. Taggart, we gotta talk, okay?"

15

FIFTEEN MINUTES LATER, THE SUN SURRENDERED TO THE
ridge line off to their west. The three men sat on logs
by a fire pit near the shack, but not too near. Taggart
had flung a cup of accelerant onto the wood stacked
like a teepee in the rock-rimmed pit. Travis caught a
whiff of kerosene... and peppermint? The old boy
struck a wooden match on the heel of his boot,
tossed it into the pit.

Whoosh!

After checking that he still had eyebrows,
Jamison said, "Mr. Taggart, we need your help."

"S'jus Taggart. Ain't no mister. Cain't do nothin'
to help you boys."

Travis said, "Sir, we think you can. The bastards that killed Frank might be working some of this turf. Hear any shooting? See anyone taking any bears? Or maybe see dead ones missing parts? They might be cutting off their heads and paws and taking their gall bladders."

"Their what?"

"Gall bladders. They're selling them for big bucks."

"How come? I mean, even I wouldn't eat *that* shit, for love 'r money.

Jamison nodded and puckered one cheek. "That's exactly it. Money for the poachers. Love tonics for the buyers. Worth more than cocaine or heroin, ounce for ounce. Get it?"

Taggart looked up from the fire, glanced sideways, first at Jamison to his left, then Travis on his other side. He said, "You boys *on* sumpin'?"

Now impatient, Travis said, "Are you gonna help us, or not?"

Taggart swiveled his gaze, snapped his filthy suspenders with his sooty thumbs and grimaced, but said nothing. Travis looked at Jamison across the fire, who jerk-nodded his head sideways with a hard squint and pursed lips. Message: *wait him out.*

Then....

"I liked that Murdock fella." Taggart stared down at the roaring fire as it crackled away, spitting its most stubborn sparks up toward the stars.

"So, how do we get in with these poachers?"

The old woodsman finally said, "Well, I been hearin' shootin' in places where I don't usually hear much. So I went down yonder ta the far side of Jeremiah's Ridge ta see what was goin' on.

"These three boys with their big hounds, wires 'n small antenna's on 'em too, well they was killin' every bear in sight up there. I thought about fixin' 'em so they wouldn't do that no more. Anyway, I just got a real bad feelin' from them boys...."

Taggart still stared at the fire as his squeaky sandpaper voice trailed off. Travis stared at Jamison, who squinted and shook his head again. Same message: *wait.*

"They ain't gcnna take too kindly ta lettin' some stranger in on their killin'." The old man squinted his right eye, pinched his lips, and clawed at his bearded neck like there might be a thought worth harvesting in there. "Hmmm, the way they take ta them dogs might be a start."

With pent-up intensity and a voice higher than usual, juiced with frustration, Travis said, "What do you mean?" He had grown tired of slow-dancing.

"Well," now the old man looked up with a glint in his cloudy eyes, "no dogs, no bears. They gotta have them dogs ta find the bears, y'unnerstand? If they was ta lose one, f'rinstance, and you found it, and brought it back," he offered Travis a sly wink so big his head bobbed, and then aimed another just like it at Jamison, "they might appreciate that, now, mightn't they?"

A slow grin crept across Jamison's stubbled face as he offered the old fox a furrowed brow on one side of his forehead and a smirk of appreciation. Both Jamison and Taggart jumped, startled by Travis blurting, "Ha! No shit, old man. That's brilliant!"

Taggart spit a syrupy blob of chaw juice onto the fire. It spit back. "Fellas, you gotta see jus' how they work them bears. 'Cause when they're huntin', see, one of 'em handles the dogs, another does the shootin', and the third one helps dressin' and carryin' out the goods. Now, if one of 'em got hurt, accidental, mind you...."

Jamison smiled, "Yes, that'd be just too bad, wouldn't it, Mr. Taggart? Any ideas where we might find their camp?"

"One ridge over from Rutledge Glen. Good cover, good water and plenty a bears ta kill."

Travis got excited about the old codger's plan.

He said a little louder than he intended, "So tell me, how do I get one of their dogs off a hot bear track?"

Taggart dragged his ear-muff cap off his mop of tangled hair, scratched the top of his head, and then rewarded both wardens with a big, almost-toothless grin—fate had spared him one or two. They thought the end of his nose might just touch the tip of his chin where it poked out of his scraggly beard.

JAMISON AND TRAVIS SAID THEIR GOODBYES TO TAGGART with good-natured grunts and half-assed salutes, stopping short of shaking hands, not knowing where they'd been, and doing God knows what. Both cops walked without speaking, deep in thought.

Halfway back to the Bronco, picking their steps with care in the semi-darkness, Travis said, "Boy, this oughta be good."

The two men approached their truck. Jamison up-nodded toward a dense stand of birches and whispered, "Check it out."

In the almost day-glow of a full moon, a magnificent trophy deer stood proud in its natural habitat less than twenty yards away. Further along the trail, a mother black bear and cub at play rolled in the grass and cuffed each other. They didn't yet know they should be afraid. Both men shook their heads sideways with unspoken sadness and disgust at what they now knew was happening beyond Jeremiah's Ridge over Rutledge way.

16

THAT NIGHT, TRAVIS, HIS SON BRIAN, AND KATE PREPARED a late dinner together in the kitchen. Brian helped Kate set the table. Travis cooked Pasta Primavera at the stove—one pot to boil the noodles, another for the veggies, and a third for his special Béchamel sauce.

Not that his recipe was anything special—although he fancied himself a damn good cook—it was his own unique variation. Always got rave reviews. The secret was cumin. Waves of fresh-minced garlic permeated the kitchen.

Kate said, "So, Brian, how's school going?"

In his best early-teen drone, he said, "Okay, I guess." Neither was eye contact his strong suit.

Still at the stove, testing the pasta and always the dad, Sam said, "Other than having some trouble with History, right, Bri?"

Kate perked up. "That was my favorite subject! Maybe I can help, Brian."

His sullen tone betrayed him. "Naw, I don't think so. I just have to study more."

Kate smiled, but worried that Brian's reluctance to look her in the eye meant their relationship was still strained.

She thought, *The poor kid misses his mom and worries that his dad is trying to replace her, and maybe him.*

Travis worried, too. He chirped with a little too much cheer, "Let's eat!"

An hour later, he perched on the edge of Brian's bed, elbows on knees, and his hands clenched together. He gazed at his son to his left lying on the bed with his face turned away.

"What's wrong, Bri?" The silence was deafening. "C'mon, son, talk to me."

100

Brian turned just his head, still reluctant to engage. Sam leaned in to hear him.

"Dad? Can I ask you something?" He sounded afraid to say the words aloud.

"Sure. Go ahead."

"Do you still miss Mom?"

"Yeah, son. I do. Every single day."

"Do you like Kate?"

"Yep."

"A lot?"

"Son, why don't you just get to the point? What's bothering you?"

Brian turned over and frowned. Swung his legs to hang over the edge of his bed. Sam understood him very well now, as his boy confronted him.

"How can you marry someone else and still love Mom?"

There it is. The boy doesn't have a clue how to think about all this. Like I do?

Sam Travis, fearless environmental cop, feared loving a woman other than his dear departed wife. He worried most that his boy was confused about all of this.

"Well, first, I didn't say anything about getting married. But loving your mom doesn't mean that I should punish myself by being alone, by not having someone like your mother to share my life with. You know that, right?

"But you're not alone, Dad. You got me."

"I know, son. Because Kate and I have a relationship doesn't take away anything. Not any of the memories, or the love your Mom and I shared, and our love for you. Because I've let Kate into my life doesn't mean we've forgotten your mother. It won't change us. Your Mom would understand, and she'd want us both to be happy. And I'd bet anything that Kate now loves you, too. So give her a chance, huh? Please try? For me?

Brian just cast his eyes toward the braided rug on the hardwood floor by his bed, swung his legs back up on the bed, and turned away without another word.

Travis ruffled his hair and padded out in his stocking feet.

As he turned left outside Brian's door and reached the head of the stairs to the living room, he looked down and saw Kate standing there. She hugged herself, cocked her head forward and to her left, worried about how *the talk* had gone. He descended and stood in front of her, rubbing her shoulders.

She said, "Thanks for dinner. Everything okay?"

"It will be."

He put one arm around her shoulder. They walked to the sofa facing the fire where they could sit close, and bask in the glow of the flames—and of each other.

17

FRIDAY,

> October 7th
> Law Enforcement Headquarters
> Boston, Massachusetts

AN EXPLOSION OF NOISE, TRAFFIC, AND PEOPLE SCURRYING
in all directions engulfed Travis and Jamison as they
entered the building through a huge revolving door.

They pushed through and headed for a bank of
elevators on the far side of the large lobby amid a
throng of folks who all needed to be somewhere else
in a hurry. They packed in like ticks in a swimming
pup's ears.

The two men exited the elevator on the thirty-eighth floor. Straight ahead, a well-dressed receptionist greeted them at the center of a circular reception area drowning in glass and ebony. Sam shivered.

"Go right in, gentlemen."

They nodded. Before they could go around the young women's desk, Commissioner Verdi met them outside the double doors to his office. Sam's first impression? He looked like a body-building politician.

Nice suit. Had to cost a frickin' bundle....

He said, "Right on time, boys. I want you to meet someone."

As they passed through the frosted glass doors with the three-foot brushed stainless handles, Travis checked out the commissioner's office. Spacious, plush, comfortable, a huge executive desk with a high-back chair behind it, and incredible leather guest chairs you could do a creamy backstroke in. The wall of glass behind the desk painted a gorgeous portrait of the Boston skyline with the Charles River and Back Bay off in the hazy distance. Million-dollar view.

Yup, the guy had style. The classy glass bookcases that lined two of the other walls were interrupted only by gilt-framed pictures that were matted and glassed. This could be the office of a college president. Or a gangster.

A slide projector perched at the far end of a mammoth green-tinted glass conference table surrounded by a dozen stylish chairs. The projector was loaded with a carousel aimed at a screen that was descending from a six-foot-long cylindrical canister mounted near the ceiling as they entered. Seemed out of place in the otherwise impeccably decorated office, like it was a necessary evil.

Commissioner Verdi led the two environmental police officers toward a well-dressed forty-ish Asian-American man with close-cropped salt-and-pepper hair—still more pepper than salt. The man stood guard over the slides in the projector.

The commissioner said, "Gentlemen, this is Agent Kim Mason from U.S. Fish and Wildlife, Special Operations. Kim has offered his assistance and expertise with the Murdock case. I'll let him explain what you might be up against. Agent Mason, this is Captain Lawrence Jamison, case supervisor, and his covert operative Sam Travis."

After curt handshakes all around, Mason said, "I called the commissioner after I saw the all-hands broadcast. The evidence found at the crime scene is consistent with what might be a commercial poaching operation.

"I can also tell you from nine years of experience that the parts taken from those bears are being sold into the Asian market. But let's start with a little show-and-tell. Commissioner, would you douse the lights, please?"

Travis thought, *Another nice suit.*

NOW SEATED BEHIND HIS DESK, COMMISSIONER VERDI pressed a button to the right of his phone console. The room dimmed, and fancy electric blinds on the wall of windows closed.

The two cops smirked at each other in a way so their big boss couldn't see. Somebody found budget for toys while *they* drove rusty old Broncos in the field equipped with ten-year-old radios and bald tires.

Jamison, Travis and Mason sat back in their seats near the head of the long table. Maybe it was his imagination, but Travis thought he saw Mason grimace at the sight of his scuffed and slightly muddy boots through the tinted table top.

Huh.

Mason turned on the slide projector that lit up the screen. The fan that cooled the high-wattage bulb began displacing its considerable heat with a steady *whir.*

Mason said, "The first slide..."

Commissioner Verdi retained custody of the projector's wired remote from his desk ten feet away. Odd.

The carousel rotated one position forward.

Click. Clunk.

"This shows seized evidence."

On the screen they all saw an open field of asphalt with officers inspecting row upon row of elephant tusks, rhinoceros horns, and deer antlers still in their velvet sleeves.

"All of this contraband was taken from a poaching ring apprehended at Kennedy Airport. The parts were labeled and found in grain bags, ticketed for Korea. Okay, next slide...."

Click. Clunk.

"Here, you see decapitated bear heads and paws. Also, these are sealed plastic packages of bear galls, lying on a table in an unidentified room. Agents seized all of this in a southeastern processing plant during a recent undercover investigation. Each set of paws, head, and gall bladder is worth ten thousand U.S. Dollars today at any port of entry in South Korea."

Both Jamison and Travis sat up straighter, looked at each other in the darkened room, and their eyes opened wider.

Jamison said, "Ten *thousand?*"

Mason nodded. The projector's carousel rotated and clicked the next slide into place. Now recognizing what they were seeing, they studied the various packages, all sizes, wrapped in gold foil.

Mason continued. "Inside is the finished product. Sold by the gram for about fourteen-hundred US, they sell the processed parts to pharmacies, doctors, whomever—domestic and overseas."

Click. Clunk.

The commissioner no longer needed a prompt to advance the slide.

"Here's a crew of five in custody. The men involved in this case are not your usual violators. The guy in the middle owns a car dealership. On the extreme right is a computer engineer, and the little fellow next to him with the glasses runs a package store. The other two are local bandits with extensive petty criminal histories—"

Travis interrupted the agent. "Are you saying shits like these murdered Frank?"

"Not necessarily. Commissioner, lights, please."

MASON LEVIED A STERN EXPRESSION TOWARD SAM. "DO not underestimate them, Officer Travis. The leader is probably well-educated, well-equipped and well-financed, with all the connections to unload the goods."

Jamison scratched his chin and said, "You mean Far East connections, right?"

"Yeah. *And* domestic. For centuries, various Far Eastern cultures have used animal parts and organs for medicinal purposes and aphrodisiacs. Now, their indigenous animals near extinction. So they've turned to rogue hunters here and made America their new killing field."

Jamison spoke up again. "How much money is involved?"

"Plenty. Millions. Heading toward billions."

Testing him, Travis said, "Agent Mason, have you had any success infiltrating these groups?"

Mason offered a thin smile. "Some. It's difficult to get anyone inside, but not impossible."

"I see. So, how can you help us?"

Mason sat down opposite Travis and Jamison. The commissioner joined them at the big table. He, too, wrinkled his forehead when he spotted Sam's boots through the tabletop.

What is it with these guys?

Mason said, "My agency will provide you with surveillance equipment, covert identities, credit cards, licenses, jobs—"

The commissioner interrupted Mason. "And all

the rest of it. Kim and I will coordinate the logistics. Kim, I can handle it from here. Anything else for the guys?"

"Nope. I'll leave you gentlemen to discuss the details. Meanwhile, thanks for your time, and if you need anything, you can reach me at my office."

As soon as the door closed behind Agent Mason, Travis swiveled his chair away from the table and toward the commissioner, now seated to his right, Jamison to his left, and waited for somebody who wasn't wearing muddy boots to say something.

Jamison ruffled his hair, maybe symbolic of clearing his head. "Amazing stuff, boss. Is Mason Japanese, Korean...?"

"Korean-American. His father was a GI killed in action in nineteen-fifty-two. His mother, a Korean, became seriously ill, could not care for him, so she sent Mason to the States to be raised by relatives."

Commissioner Verdi flipped open a manila folder to read its contents. "Grew up in Los Angeles, graduated UCLA with honors, and joined the Wildlife Feds in 1975. Lots of achievement awards since. Special Ops unit for eight years now."

He snapped the folder closed as if he had just revealed all the guys needed to know.

"The man himself...." Verdi shrugged. "Look, you

two are neophytes in this kind of operation. Mason's experience might give you an edge."

Travis scratched the back of his neck, stared down at the folder on the glass table, shook his head from side to side. He said, "My gut tells me we oughta go slow with this... develop our leads before—"

Verdi jumped in. "What leads?"

Jamison oozed with mock enthusiasm in mediocre but staunch support of his junior officer's judgment. "None, sir. But we're working on it." He rolled his eyeballs, then wrinkled his forehead with an icy glare swiveled toward Travis.

Verdi picked up on Jamison's reaction. He said, "Okay. I want to be briefed as soon as you have anything."

OUT IN THE HALLWAY EN ROUTE TO THE ELEVATORS, TRAVIS said, "What's goin' on, boss?"

"I think you should let me do the talking when we're in that office."

"What did I say?"

"Enough to bother me. The less Verdi knows, the better. At least for now."

Travis ignored the intimation and just punched the down button harder than necessary.

I'm why they stress-test these damn buttons, he thought.

They stepped into the first car to arrive. Stood on opposite sides, both lost in thought, not looking each other in the eye.

18

Travis pulled his Bronco into the strip mall's parking lot. He slid out, walked to the front door labeled,

*American Society
for the Prevention of
Cruelty to Animals*

It swung outward, of course.
He could tell right away the young man behind

the desk was going to be trouble. He seemed patronizing, even from across the room. With all the constant barking, the kid had to love working in this smelly, noisy place. Travis noticed he sported five Band-Aids—on his fingers and arms—festooned with cartoon characters. High-camp humor? Four of the five appeared fresh. The fifth, not so much.

What's with all the barking and yelping and whining? Not happy to be here. I wouldn't be. Or they remembered where they came from.

With these thoughts floating through his consciousness, Travis scanned the waiting area. Scoped out the four folks sitting there. No apparent threats. Travis approached the kid in coveralls who was talking to someone on the phone. But he watched Travis nearing *his* counter. Just another animal lover.

Travis wore civilian clothes: a baseball cap, faded jeans, and a t-shirt that said:

> *I'd throw you in front of a zombie*
> *to protect my German Shepherd.*

"... Yes, we've given her the shots... you can pick her up anytime... you're welcome, ma'am."

The kid hung up the phone, never having taken

GK JURRENS

his eyes off Travis. He said, "Yes, sir. Cool shirt. Can I help you?"

Bashful, Travis said, "I'm looking for a bitch in heat."

The guy smiled. He'd heard it before.

Travis added, "I only need her for the afternoon."

The kid tugged at his chin, sporting maybe half a dozen peach-fuzz hairs. Travis would bet he called those sprouts a goatee. Still keeping his eyes on Travis, the kid shouted over his shoulder to an invisible party behind the swinging doors to his rear. But now he reinforced his words with a lascivious leer, still studying Travis from head to toe.

"Hey Bobby! Your ex-wife still in town?"

Both male pet owners in the waiting area suppressed chuckles. Even an old man sitting there. The two women only looked startled and offended at this little prick's thoughtless joke.

Embarrassed, and without saying another word, Travis hung his head and shook it from side to side. He slantwise glanced up at the little prick's still-leering face who remained amused at his own tired and offensive humor.

Travis slapped his right hand on the counter, nodded, straightened up and walked out, disgusted.

· · ·

GLENVILLE, MASSACHUSETTS
Burlington Mall

SHOPS DISPLAYED EVERYTHING FROM LEISURE-WARE TO sporting goods to appliances. Shoppers browsed and strolled. Some nibbled on confectionary or other disgusting snacks and drinks. Most toted parcels and bags with bright store logos on their sides. The mood felt festive.

A pet store window displayed rows of cages with puppies cavorting or sleeping on an aromatic bed of cedar chips. Travis tromped in and aimed his gait toward the attractive blonde standing behind the store's short counter.

The smells of animals and cedar and fish and ozone from the aquariums assaulted his senses. This place was even noisier than the animal shelter. But the counter girl looked happy to see him.

At first.

Travis had learned his lesson. Or so he thought. Without offending anyone, how *do* you ask for a female dog in heat that you only needed for one day? As soon as he inquired, though, the girl still grew offended. Her smile turned into a sneer as she obviously jumped to the wrong conclusion. Then her face flushed with anger.

She said, shaking with emotion, "Please, just leave." She had even stopped chewing her gum, maybe even swallowed it. *And* she pointed to the door, as if he needed directions.

Fuck!

Once more, he slunk out, embarrassed and defeated.

19

WEDGWOOD, MASSACHUSETTS

TRAVIS SLUMPED IN A WINDOW BOOTH OF THE Wedgewood Diner.

Regulars occupied their customary swivel stools at the counter—the smoking section. Like second-hand smoke stopped shy of the booths, the non-smoking section, right behind them, right?. Sam shook his head at the outrageous notion that everyone seemed to think was perfectly logical.

The diner was noisy, as always. But the shouted orders always amused him. He welcomed the distraction and enjoyed testing his knowledge of diner lingo.

The same waitress who served him and Jamison the other day—he made the mistake of calling her a *server,* but only once—hoofed behind the counter to clip her green and white order slip with an abrupt vertical thrust to the short-order cook's turnstile.

She hollered through the window to the grill, "One hockey puck painted yellow, hold the grass, whistle berries and frog sticks in the alley!"

Travis smiled. *A well-done hamburger with mustard, no lettuce, with side orders of baked beans and French fries.*

Ten seconds later, one cook hollered out from the smoky kitchen, "Sandy, eight's up. Adam 'n Eve on a raft, extra cow paste, Jayne Mansfield drowned in machine oil!"

Two poached eggs on toast, lots of butter, twin stacks of flapjacks doused in syrup. Of course.

While he decoded the boisterous diner slang between two "servers" and a pair of fry cooks, Travis swirled a spoon in his coffee. He had finally gotten it to just the right color. Used to drink it good 'n black, but his stomach bitched at him now when he back-slid to his old sinful ways.

An older man approached like a friendly stranger, swung into the booth across from Travis without being invited. Before Travis could object, the grizzled codger growled something out. A satisfied grin spread across Travis's face. He was the old man from the Glenville ASPCA waiting room!

FIFTEEN MINUTES LATER, TRAVIS STROLLED FROM HIS Bronco to a junkyard just south of town. The place reeked of old motor oil and wet rust. Weeds had conquered the ground between stacks of smashed cars and trucks. They also grew up the center of short piles of tires that had been around a long time. Loud machinery ground away from somewhere inside a dilapidated building toward the back of the property.

Yup, a typical junkyard going to seed.

The old man from the diner—the ASPCA guy— was also the tobacco-spitting owner of this establishment. Without saying a word, Travis nodded and stuffed some wrinkled bills into his calloused and cracked hand. He motioned Travis to follow him.

Some twenty yards from what might have once been a guard shack before it partially collapsed, they approached a rusty van on its axles. Minus wheels and tires, the axles dug into a patch of weedy sand. The yard owner swung open the van's rear doors with a flourish.

A startled Doberman Pincer started snarling—

lips curled, with teeth flashing. The dog tugged against a choker collar chained and shackled to a tool rack inside the van. Travis recoiled and tripped over a weather-cracked tire engulfed in the weed patch behind him. But he did not go down.

"Jeezus H!"

The old man spoke. Sounded like he'd been smoking Pall Mall straights for sixty years.

He spit a cheek full of brown juice, hitting the center of the tire Travis had tripped over. Wiped renegade drips from his beard with the back of his left sleeve, already stained black from carefree earlier target practice.

"Meet Jezebel. G'wan, pet her. She won't bite."

"Hell, she won't!"

"No problem, son. Just let 'er smell yer hand."

"*Eat* my hand is more like it."

Travis stepped forward. Despite the abject fear on his face, the dog settled down. Sniffed the back of his hand. Just in case, Travis protected his fingers with a closed fist.

"See, Jezebel's in love with you's already."

He laughed through the chunks of gravel in his voice box and a protracted bout of coughing. Slapped Travis on the back even as he hunched over to cough out a piece of at least one lung. Or so it seemed.

Once he recovered, he unleashed Jezebel, who immediately rubbed her aching loins against his legs. Travis appreciated this find and handed the owner a few more small bills.

Now on a leather leash to replace the chain, game warden and antsy dog traipsed off to said warden's Bronco.

20

———

Armed with his list, Travis mentally ticked off his supplies as he touched each item:

Let's see... rifles, three boxes of ammo, camping gear, food, supplies, and seized black bear carcasses from the frozen evidence locker....

He loaded it all into the back of this "new" truck, inside the bed's locking topper. Already stunk in there. Jezebel looked on from within the dog carrier inside the topper, now and then emitting quick barks of excitement.

Jamison tossed in some heavier gear. As he

threw Travis a set of keys to this "clean" truck—courtesy of Agent Mason, he said, "Here ya go. Hey, some decent wheels, right? Here's your fake ID and credit cards, also courtesy of the feds. Ready to rock?"

"Let's do this."

OCTOBER MOUNTAIN

JAMISON FOLLOWED TRAVIS IN HIS "NEW" THREE-quarter-ton undercover truck. She'd been rode hard and put away wet. This beat-up, blacked-out, eight-year-old, four-wheel-drive Dodge Power Wagon was supplied by the feds with a clean history.

Damn-near took a ladder to get in and out of this diesel rig, though. And not exactly a smooth ride. She sat atop a six-inch lift kit over Ironman All Country tires with Bilstein shocks.

The fiberglass topper over its short bed looked funky, but was perfect for concealing contraband while rolling down the road. She was a stout rig, alright. A poacher's rig.

It only took forty minutes to reach the isolated ridge old Taggart had identified as a likely area for the poachers' activity. Jezebel needed to relieve herself. Travis looped her leash back onto itself around a small tree, reconnected her, and went to work.

AFTER PARKING HIS OWN TRUCK, JAMISON WALKED THE perimeter for signs of any human activity.

Twenty minutes later, Travis had set up camp. He'd pitched his tent and laid out his provisions, just the way he liked them, including his relatively fresh contraband—his bona fides.

Jamison emerged from the woods and walked over to say goodbye.

He said, "I don't want to find you like you found Murdock. With no communications, I won't be able to bail your ass out, so be careful."

"Don't worry, boss. I'll meet you at the crossroad.

As Jamison's truck rumbled down the trail the way they had come, Travis freed Jezebel's leash from the tree near his tent and said, "Let's go, girl."

He had shortened her leash with several loops around his forearm for better control. He'd gotten very comfortable with her. She was a good girl. Just horny as hell.

Travis led her all around the area so that her

coital scent would permeate the ambush site. She peed. A *lot*. Good. Led Jezebel the short distance back to his truck, secured her in the cage inside the topper, checked his revolver and headed back the thirty yards to his campsite.

He laid a trip wire across the trail tied to a tree on one side and positioned himself behind a fallen tree with a firm grip on the other end. Camouflaged under a light layer of forest debris, he waited. A warm afternoon sun twinkled down through falling leaves, and beamed past the ones that still clung to their branches.

A half-hour later, the sound of a twig snapping close by caused Travis to raise his head with caution. He spotted a black bear with her two cubs. All three stood there, nervous, their nostrils flaring, not twenty yards away.

A QUARTER MILE AWAY, A BLUE TICK HOUND FOLLOWED HIS nose, hot on the hunt. He bayed with enthusiasm as he ran, dropping his nose every ten yards to sniff the trail. Filled his lungs with fresh bear scent. He ran faster.

MEANWHILE, TRAVIS MARVELED AT A WIDE SCAR ACROSS the big sow's nose as she looked after her frolicking cubs. In his mind, he named her *Scarface*. They relaxed and just enjoyed the warm day.

But Travis flipped to full alert when he heard the persistent baying of a strike dog getting nearer and nearer, louder and louder. He sat bolt upright.

Got the bears' attention. Mom's, at least. Travis helped spur Scarface into action and hissed, "Git!"

The sow jumped to his warning. She growled and lumbered off with her cubs.

THE STRIKE DOG WAS NOW PAIRED WITH A RED-BONE hound, both eager to track the powerful scent with their noses fanning the air now as often as the ground ahead of them.

A half-mile further back on the trail, four more dogs that clipped along at the same pace led their bearded handler. He spotted a brighter area ahead that promised the glimmer of an open clearing and a clean chase.

Two men in head-to-toe camouflage farther back moved faster now, cradling rifles to their chests.

21

THE BLUE TICK AND THE RED BONE APPROACHED TO WITHIN fifteen feet of Travis's hide when the hounds caught Jezebel's scent and chased it with boyish enthusiasm, forgetting the bears.

Travis crawled out of his improvised hide and closed in behind them. He knew they now followed their *little* heads.

Inside the carrier in the covered truck bed, Jezebel awaited her suitors. The two hounds did not hesitate. They leaped onto the pickup's open tailgate and slid into the topper's interior, sniffing and panting and pawing at Jezebel's locked cage. They gave no consideration to Travis approaching the truck at a run.

GK JURRENS

He snapped the tailgate shut and closed the topper's lid all in one motion. Hopped into the cab, cranked the engine, popped her into drive, and drove just fifty yards down the trail to a secluded spot in a copse of birch trees. He then ran as fast as he could back to the ambush site. Crouched behind the fallen tree again and waited—watching and listening.

Travis heard before he saw the young bearded man in dungarees and a mackinaw jacket who took no precaution to be quiet. His boots crunched branches with every step. He stopped on the trail thirty feet from Travis. Took a swig from his canteen, spit and looked around, disgusted. He whistled. Nothing. Spit again.

Travis ducked lower. The poacher capped his canteen, then moved off down the trail at a rapid pace. Travis tightened his grip on the loose end of the slack trip wire. As the poacher approached it, he quick-jerked it taut.

The wire caught the poacher across the joint between foot and ankle. The guy went flying. Travis thanked the gods of fate as the poacher struck his forehead on a jagged rock alongside the trail. Knocked him unconscious.

Travis approached, holding a four-foot branch over his shoulder like a club. Satisfied that the poacher was unconscious, he whacked him hard across the knee. A groan leaked out even though he was still out cold.

Said, "That's for the bears, you asshole."

Travis turned to walk away, but hesitated. Returned to the still-unconscious poacher. Was that the stench of urine coming off this redneck in waves? Gave him another solid *thud* with his boot to the ribs.

"This one's for scarin' those cubs! And take a damn shower!"

The poacher's leg twitched. He let out a low, aching moan.

22

THE CROSSROAD

TRAVIS ARRIVED IN HIS "NEW" TRUCK TO MEET JAMISON IN his. He tossed his boss a casual thumbs-up out the window as he approached. They parked side by side, and he transferred Jezebel into Jamison's truck.

No conversation.

The two hounds that remained with Travis howled in protest. After exchanging casual salutes, Jamison headed south. Travis aimed his truck north and hit the gas sufficient to spin those gnarly mud tires on the gravel.

No time to waste.

With the truck parked back at his campsite,

Travis led the poachers' two dogs through a break in the sixty-foot oaks , now in all their autumn splendor. A couple nights of near freezes'll do that.

MEANWHILE, A MAN WATCHED HIM SOME FIFTY YARDS distant through the crosshairs of his large-bore rifle. Spotted the two familiar hounds, and lowered his weapon as the stranger hiked toward his concealed location. He waited.

When the grizzly young man got close, still leading the two dogs straining at their leashes, the poacher popped cut onto the trail in front of him.

TRAVIS ALMOST BUMPED INTO THE HULK WHO materialized out of the brush onto the trail. The hounds stopped tugging on their leashes and circled the guy dressed in full camo.

The mountain of a man cradled a Ruger Bushmaster 450 rifle with a Night Force SHV scope across his barrel chest. Serious firepower that looked small in his hands. This guy could be a professional wrestler with biceps exceeding the circumference of your average teenage girl's waist.

The guy's voice rumbled. "Lost?"

"Nope. Just looking for the guy who owns these hounds."

Suspicion creased the monster's forehead made larger with a shaved head and no hat. Upon closer inspection, this guy looked like a pro wrestler who had gone to seed. Those forehead creases were folds of fat, not skin on bone.

He said, "Where'd you find 'em?"

"They came into my camp earlier this afternoon, whipped, wet, and hungry."

"Yeah, well, they belong to me and my buddies. We got a camp over by the lake. So I'll take 'em back now. You carryin'?"

Travis took a beat to look this guy in the eye. He drew back his unbuttoned jacket to reveal a shoulder-holstered three-fifty-seven. Said, "Yeah, what's the problem?"

"The *problem* is, I don't know who the fuck you are."

A cold bead of sweat roll down Travis's back under an already clammy shirt and a jacket too heavy for the afternoon air. It had been colder this morning.

Moment of truth, or just the opposite. His expression had started out with an open and friendly smile—one hunter to another. Now, his lips tightened, along with the grip on the dogs' leashes. He leaned his head back at an angle and studied this asshole in front of him with pursed lips.

"And I don't know who the fuck *you* are, either. Just show me some proof that they're your dogs and I'm outta here."

The poacher's knuckles whitened around the barrel grip of his rifle, but hoisted a smile that didn't even come close to reaching his eye slits.

"Sure, pal. The collar frequency is one-five-three-point-nine-six. Go ahead. Check it."

Travis reeled in one dog's leash, squatted and squinted as he read the engraved frequency on the little silver plate riveted to his leather collar.

He stood and nodded, but said nothing. His clamped jaw jutted forward broadcast he didn't much care for this asshole's gruff attitude when all he was offering was a kindness by returning the fucker's dogs. Travis was all-in-character.

THE POACHER'S DEMEANOR SOFTENED. HE SAID, "LOOK, I do 'preciate the return, mister. Sorry if I sounded a little rough."

Travis stared at him. After a couple of seconds,

like he was taking his time to decide whether to stay pissed, he handed over the dogs.

"That's better. Name's Russ Baker. I own a garage over on Route 47. I *do* need those leashes back."

The guy smiled. A little. "Randy Sackett's the name. You might've heard of me. Used to be a pro wrestler. Anyway, I was just being careful. No hard feelings, okay?"

Sackett waited for a response. Travis didn't give him the satisfaction.

"So what are you doin' out here besides walkin' dogs?"

"Some pre-season scouting for bears."

Then, and only then, did Travis, a.k.a. Baker, offer Sackett his hand. The brute's mitt was a study of massive strength and size.

Sackett released him while Travis did his best not to wince at the residual pain while he waited for the blood to return to his hand.

"How about a drink? C'mon, meet the guys."

Travis paused. Didn't want to appear too eager. Son-of-a-bitch if old Taggart's plan wasn't working. Then....

"Yeah, why not? I'm in a hurry to go nowhere, anyway."

• • •

THEY HIKED FOR THIRTY MINUTES. SACKETT LED THE WAY. Dusk approached as they came upon a camp with a fire already blazing in front of two side-by-side tents.

The guy Travis had taken down with his trip wire and kicked shit out of while he was unconscious was already there and wrapped in a sleeping bag. Appeared to be dozing.

Another scruffy-looking bastard stood nearby. Both he and his rifle leaned against a tree. Travis spotted four more bear hounds leashed to a wire run that were alerted to Travis and Sackett as they shuffled into camp with the other two hounds.

The scruffy bastard—a wiry runt—had killer eyes. No longer leaning, he reached for his rifle by its barrel and said, "Who's your friend, Sackett?"

"Found him on the trail with our dogs, Charlie. Name's Russ Baker. And says he's got baits out."

The scruffy runt said with menace in his voice, "You're better than that, Randy."

"Easy, Charlie. This guy did us a favor, so I invited him for a drink. No harm done."

23

TRAVIS BROKE IN ON THIS LITTLE DANCE. "NICE LITTLE operation." He swept his gaze around the camp. "Doesn't take a genius to figure out what you got here.

"First, it ain't bear season. Second, you got all that radio shit on your dogs. Another thing is all that equipment and firepower."

With his left thumb hooked in his belt, he pointed around with his right hand.

"So I guess you guys are my competition to clean out my fuckin' bears."

Charlie sneered at him. "*Your* bears? What are you... their daddy or somethin'?"

Travis pulled his thumb from his belt. Both arms

dropped to his sides, like he was about to pull a John Wayne on this prick. He spoke with heat in his voice, but at a low volume, which only made it sound more menacing.

"Hey, my family's been takin' bear and deer out of these hills for fifty fuckin' years. Besides, I know every local around, and you ain't any of 'em. And neither is Paul Bunyan here."

He tossed a slantwise glance up toward Sackett, followed by a shifting of just one eyebrow. As if daring them to challenge the truth or severity of his words.

Then Travis glanced down at Sleeping Beauty in the bedroll by the fire. He looked back at scruffy Charlie, then at Paul Bunyan. For a full thirty seconds of tense silence. the three of them stared at each other.

THE FIRE CRACKLING BETWEEN THEM STARTED TO SMOKE and pop. Wet wood.

Mean Eyes leaned his rifle back against the tree and said, "I'm Charlie Hudson. This lame fuck," he jerked his head down toward the man in the sleeping bag who was now awake, "is Tony McRae."

McRae grinned, and the tension eased as he sat

up with grunts and winces of pain. They all snickered.

Travis thought, *What a bunch of scumbags!* But he reminded himself these could be the assholes who ended Murdock.

Travis said, "What happened to him?" He never took his eyes off scruffy Charlie Hudson, but nodded toward McRae, who had unzipped his bag and nursed what must have been some busted ribs.

McRae said, "I slipped on a banana peel." Now he rubbed his bandaged left leg.

Travis grinned, but not for the reason McRae thought. He said, "Hey, let's start fresh. I've got ten baits out and three bears in. How you guys doin'?"

Hudson said, "Pretty good, but we need a few more."

They all sat down on logs around the fire. Sackett whittled a stick, felt the tip, and said, "That's right. So what say we use Russ here? I mean, Tony's gonna to be laid up a while and we need a dog handler."

Hudson peered at him. Said, "Ever handle good bear dogs, Baker?"

"Grew up with 'em. Lost mine in Texas Hold 'Em last year. I was... under the influence."

A few thoughtful moments later and an eye-roll at McRae nursing his leg, Hudson spoke. "Okay,

Baker, if you're interested, I'd be willing to cut you in for a piece of the action while Tony's out. Just a word of caution: if you cross us, you'll regret it all the days of your short life."

The threat rolled off Travis like facts off a politician. "I'm just a good 'ol boy looking for some fun and a little extra money."

A FEELING OF WARY CAUTION BUILT. TRUST ALWAYS CAME hard. They passed a bottle around and discussed the next day's hunt. An hour later, Sackett tossed a spare bedroll to Travis.

Nobody slept.

For the longest while.

24

THE FOLLOWING MORNING, THE SMELL OF CAMPFIRE coffee awakened Travis. A blinding sunrise reflected off the lake like a mirror on fire.

Sackett was awake, but still had sleep snot in his eyes. Emerging from the tent stretching and yawning, he couldn't hide his massive torso as it rippled under his T-shirt. He wore an extra twenty or thirty pounds pretty well. Good insulation against the still but chilly morning.

McRae was still in the tent. Hudson already slouched near a respectable fire. The hounds strained at their run. They itched for another chase.

Travis had followed Sackett out of that tent's now-hooked-up flap. Buttoned his jacket, then sat with the two poachers in front of the camp stove at right angles to each other on old logs. He joined them after a mighty stretch.

Hudson asked, "What's with Tony?"

Sackett rolled his eyes. Said, "Lots of swelling. He ain't goin' far today.

Hudson shock his head and slouched some more. Looked up at the taller Travis and said, "Like we figured. No matter, we're all set with Russ here. You know what to do?"

Travis said nothing, but nodded.

Hudson reached for what looked like an over-sized gun case. He unzipped it, pulled out a crossbow and a handful of arrows—bolts. Each bolt was tipped with a razor-sharp broad-head. Attached to the gun-metal crossbow with a flat-camo composite stock was a laser scope—a frightening piece of flesh-shredding hardware.

Travis nodded toward the weapon and said, "That's pretty interesting."

Hudson sneered with pride. "Wicked is more like it. This baby will drive bolts into a three-inch circle at a hundred yards. Silent, and no need for light."

He turned on the laser as Travis eyed that hardware with morbid fascination. A bright red dot appeared on the top of his knee. Felt a flash of adrenaline course through his system.

Hudson stood and said, "See that dead tree limb?" Travis stood, too.

He pointed to a broken and dangling limb of an ancient Beech tree. Had to be almost a hundred yards out. Travis just stared ahead with folded arms and waited. Tried to look only half-interested. Hudson brought the crossbow to his shoulder and aimed. The laser projected a red dot on the limb.

Even though he knew what was coming, Travis jumped at the abrupt *clack-whoosh*.

More startling was the dead accuracy of that almost silent shot.

Crack!

The limb splintered with chunks flying as the explosive impact echoed through the trees in the quiet forest.

Sackett said under his breath, "Deadly."

He seemed to enjoy seeing Travis drop his jaw and leave it there. The fat ex-wrestler chuckled— cackled, was more like it.

The sound of evil.

Hudson hiked out to retrieve his bolt.

BUCK, THE LEAD DOG CALLED THE STRIKE DOG, TROTTED along. He worked hard, swiveling his nose in arcs in front of him as he ran. After ten minutes of relative silence, Buck erupted into a high-decibel rolling howl—a chilling, primitive call.

And the chase was on.

Further back on the trail, the trio of men jumped to high alert. Travis and the two poachers heard Buck's call. The rest of the dog pack restrained by three leashes in each of Travis's hands now fought to break free. They howled in unison as they jerked to join Buck in the hunt.

Hudson hollered, "Let 'em go!"

The pack launched into action. The whirl of fur and muscle vanished into the underbrush, the din of their yammering diminishing with distance.

25

A SPARKLING BLUE SKY SHONE WITH THE NEW DAY'S optimism and serenity above a downward-sloping ridge.

A sow bear meandered a few yards ahead of her cubs. They snorted as they rooted out bugs and other small creatures that had taken refuge under a layer of decaying wood from a blowdown. The scent lent tranquility to the setting.

Now they heard the baying hounds. Still not sure if this spelled danger, the mother bear hoisted her head, and smelled the air. Everything changed in an instant. She bounded forward in a sudden panic. The cubs sensed Mom's alarm and followed close behind.

THE PACK OF SNARLING DOGS EMERGED FROM THE BRUSH. They circled in the small meadow occupied by the trio of bears moments earlier. They sought to recapture the freshest scent of the day.

The pack once again rushed off, fanning their flaring nostrils, a savage glint in every one of their twelve eyes. A furious scramble ensued through the dense woods. They jumped over logs, under brush, and nearly flew over a rushing brook. They *knew* they were close.

The sow scurried up a tall beech tree, secured herself on a limb about fifty feet above the ground. One of her cubs on a lower limb of the same tree clung to false safety as it shivered in fear, emitting a pitiable yowl that sounded like a wounded calf. The second cub took refuge in another tree close by.

The hounds spotted them overhead, snarling, howling, and yammering as if *they* were in pain. They leaped at the base of the trees to get at the trio of bears. Tried scrambling up the trunks, their nails clattering against the bark. Their frustration mounted, as did the volume and rapidity of their cries.

· · ·

Travis and the poachers approached, sweating and breathing heavily from the effort of matching the dog pack's frenetic pace. Exhilaration gleamed in Sackett's and Hudson's eyes, dread in Travis's. He knew what must happen next.

Hudson shouted above the chaos. "Tie off some of them dogs!"

Travis tied three of the six to a tree and rejoined the two poachers. He stood there, looking up at the bears in jut-jawed silence.

Meanwhile, Sackett and Hudson un-shouldered their weapons. Hudson loaded one of those wicked bolts into his crossbow from a quiver he wore like a holster. A well-practiced routine.

Hudson winked at Travis and said, "This is the fun part."

He took aim and shot a bolt at the lone cub, silently penetrating his rear quarter. The cub's rear legs were rendered useless as it yelped and then screamed in agony. He hugged the limb with his front legs, now bawling in pathetic desperation.

Sackett was ecstatic. "Again, Charlie!" And there was that evil cackle again. Like a demon spawn's orgasm.

The second bolt struck the cub's neck, impaling it to the tree, killing it. The cub's death gurgle could be heard from the ground. A small river of blood poured down from the wound and dripped at Travis's feet.

Hudson reloaded in seconds and impaled the second cub through its chest. Travis drew his gun, a glimpse of disgust on his face. He aimed at the cub to end its suffering as quickly as possible. From his peripheral vision, he sensed Hudson facing him with the crossbow reloaded and pointed at his own head.

Hudson said, "Put that down. He's mine."

With deliberate reluctance, Travis slid his gun back into its holster.

Hudson crafted a contemptuous leer. "Don't ya like the killin', Baker boy?"

The sow now responded to the cries of her wounded cub.

Sackett released the safety on his rifle with a muted *snick*. He shouted, "She's coming down!"

Hudson chuckled. Said with flat glee, "Don't want to shoot her yet! I still wanna play—"

But the big bear was faster than Hudson expected. He drilled the sow as she almost came down from the tree on top of him. That razor-sharp broad-head bolt tore through her neck with devastating effect.

She fell to the ground, now several hundred pounds of dead weight. The dogs pounced on her lifeless body. Her second cub, already hit in the tree, let go of the limb as another bolt penetrated one side of his shoulder and continued through his body.

Travis suffered through an agonizing moment as the cub slid down, its life ebbing, breaking brittle branches, claws scrabbling in vain, and ended its fall as the little guy crashed to the ground, dead.

HUDSON AND SACKETT secured their weapons over their shoulders.

Hudson snarled at Travis. "Get these dogs outta here so we can work."

Travis barely restrained his anger, but stepped into the middle of the crazed pack. He grabbed their collars and threw them off the bears' carcasses.

Then, once he'd broken the killing spell that had washed over them, he leashed all six to an adjacent tree. Sat down on the ground and hung his head. Mopped his brow with his hat in his hand, as if tired instead of nauseated.

Gotta stay in character here, Trav. At least for now.

Every dog's muzzle was drenched in blood. So were his hands. He stifled a sob, disguising it in a mad laugh of exhilaration.

Hudson said maybe a lot louder than he

intended, "Check out the gall from this baby! Ha! Goddamn, this'll bring beaucoup bucks!"

His bloodlust gave him a crazed look.

"Get the saw, Sackett. Hey Baker! C'mon, give us a hand!"

26

KATE CALLED FROM HER DESK IN THE COURIER NEWSROOM. She paced while maneuvering around the phone's knotted cord.

"Hi, Captain Jamison? This is Kate Miller. Sam told me to call you if I had questions about the Murdock case."

"Hello, Kate. And it's just Larry. Shoot."

"Oh, okay. Well, Larry, I'm heading to New York this afternoon for a followup piece on a story. My sources tell me there's a shop in Chinatown that sells animal parts from bears, elephants, rhinos, tigers, the works. But what can they sell legally?"

She listened for thirty seconds. "Really! Terrific! You can read the story in the Courier. Okay, sure, I'll share with you what I find out. Seen Travis?"

"Sorry."

"Have him call me when you hear from him?"

She hung up, reflecting a bit before gathering a notebook, a small camera, and her soccer-ball-sized pocketbook.

THE POACHERS AND TRAVIS ARRIVED WITH THE DOGS. THEY were all tired and beat. Not smelling fresh as daisies, either.

The men had worked their way near Travis's camp and spent the night there rather than make their way back to Rutledge Glen.

Looking around, Hudson said, "Very nice, Baker. Where's your animals?"

Travis felt he was being scrutinized. "For Christ's sake, you need to know that right this minute? Let's get fuckin' unpacked first."

Hudson squinted and backed up a step, like he feared getting socked in the nose.

"Boy, you are a testy son-of-a-bitch!"

"Hudson, let's get something straight. I'm working *with* you, not *for* you. Besides, I don't like the idea of being ordered around like one of your boys. So, let's stop the bullshit. It's business, man. That's all."

Travis ended the conversation with a casual swipe of his hand, like he was swatting a blood-sucking mosquito away from his face.

Hudson said, "Fair enough. We'll unpack and then when your highness is good and ready, we'll look at your animals."

———

SACKETT KNEELED TEN FEET AWAY, UNPACKING HIS backpack. He heard the conversation. It bothered him. He scowled to himself and walked toward Travis's black monster truck. Opened the passenger door. Curious, but he made sure Baker didn't notice him.

In the glove box, just above shoulder level, he grabbed the truck's registration papers listing the name of Russ Baker, his Wedgewood address, and his vehicle ID number. He snatched a stubby little pencil out of his pocket and scribbled the numbers on the inside of a matchbook.

Sackett then returned to the campground and whittled a pointed stick waiting for Travis and Hudson to return from viewing today's kills.

He muttered under his breath, *We'll see if you're who you say you are, Mr. Baker.*

27

THE NARROW STREETS, SHOPS AND RESTAURANTS comprised a collage of movement, sound, color, odors, and most of all, congestion. Kate Miller strolled along, eyes trained straight ahead, her notebook clutched in her left hand bulging from the pencil buried inside. Her camera and pocketbook hid inside her shoulder purse.

The city could be dangerous. She made sure she didn't accidentally look anyone in the eye. You never knew. But she felt safer in Chinatown for no good reason. Still....

She stopped to peer at a shop's window display in an alley just off Doyers Street. A collection of exotic figurines and books caught her attention. Then, she seemed captivated by an arrangement of ointments, powders, and vials of colored liquids.

This was the place.

She walked inside, and the tinkle of a bell overhead announced her presence. Her nose twitched at the combination of surprising odors that assaulted her. The small store suddenly felt even smaller inside. The main aisle with a glass countertop to her left ran the entire length of the deep but narrow shop. She almost found it necessary to walk sideways. The aisle was that narrow. The twelve-foot ceiling helped. A little.

To her right, she noted row after row of wooden drawers filled with exotic medicines, herbs, lotions, and what appeared to be animal parts when she peeked into several. But the drawers were unlabeled. They lined the walls all the way to the ceiling with shelves in front of and underneath them, which also contained various vials and bottles.

Standing behind the narrow counter stood what appeared to be the proprietor. He was a Chinese man with a kind face. His spectacles perched down toward the tip of his flat nose. He seemed undisturbed as Kate entered and poked around, handling and smelling this and that.

The man finally lifted his head, saw Kate, nodded, bowed, and whispered with an accent so heavy it took Kate a moment to parse his words.

"May I help you find something, please?" The last word came out *preeze*.

What is it with Chinese and their 'L's? He seems nice.

But then she acknowledged to herself she didn't know any Chinese folk other than movie stereotypes.

Kate extended her hand. "Yes. I'm Kate Miller from the Wedgewood Courier. I'm doing a story on Oriental folk medicine. Can I ask you a few questions?"

The old gentleman took her hand and bowed again. He seemed pleased by the attention, although he likely had no clue where Wedgwood was.

"Ah, of course. I am Lu Chang. What may I share with you?"

"Well, there's so much I don't recognize, but I've heard that some things you have displayed in the window are used to cure different ailments?" A statement meant to sound like a question. An old reporter's technique.

Chang said, "An ancient tradition. We revere our doctors as practitioners endowed with the power to cure all ills. In fact, the common Chinese traditional saying is, if any part of your body is weak, you eat the equivalent animal part and it will help you."

She wrote that down, fascinated, and asked, "Mr. Chang, are some of these remedies used to improve one's sex life?"

The left corner of the old man's silky-whiskered mouth migrated closer to his now-twinkling eyes. "Beautiful lady, of course. It is a minor aspect; however, we have certain aids like rhinoceros horn and tiger penis which will help restore or improve sexual competency."

Kate blushed, despite her professional fortitude. "That's good to know. Um, how much would one pay for these aids?"

"The prices vary, according to the amounts required, also the frequency. May I show you?"

"Please. That would be helpful."

Chang removed some gold foil-wrapped packages from a middle drawer against the back wall. It was dark so far from the shop's front windows He then opened one on the counter to reveal a gum-ball-sized, tan-colored pill. He placed it in her hand.

Chang said, "This is ground rhino horn. Rare,

and very expensive. Today, you may have it for one thousand dollars."

As a reflex, Kate shoved the gum-ball back into Chang's hand. "Whew! Tell me, Mr. Chang, isn't this illegal? And who supplies you with these?"

Chang accepted the rhino horn ball from her, lowered his eyes, and said, "I cannot tell you that for obvious reasons, Miss Miller. As you must know, we have our difficulties from time to time with your authorities. Nevertheless, the traditions survive."

He lifted his eyes and offered her what seemed to be a genuine and sincere smile.

Kate's gaze wandered at the complexity and closeness of her surrounding. She had never smelled such a combination of odors. Offering Chang a smile of her own and a head shake of admiration at the extent and diversity of his unusual inventory, she said, "I see. Well, it's been an education, and I so appreciate your candor. May I take your picture?"

Chang said, "I would be honored."

Kate stepped back with her camera to focus on Lu Chang who now stood closer to the store's front. She liked the gauzy late afternoon light coming from the store's windows. Chang struck a pose behind the counter.

Just then, the door opened and a shadowy figure

approached Chang. He passed through her camera's field of view as she snapped the picture before he turned and left again. With a suspicious abruptness.

Curious.

28

IT WAS AFTER NINE. KATE WAS ON A MISSION. SHE WALKED toward the photo lab to find Jerry Benjamin putting on his coat. He was just about to give up on her after promising to wait for her return from the city.

Out of breath, Kate huffed. "Sorry I'm late, Jerry darlin'. Here's the film." She flipped the exposed roll to him. He caught it and used that same hand to point back at her with a faux frown.

He said, "Just remember, I'm only doing this because you've got great legs."

They both smirked. Jerry was harmless. He took off his coat again and returned to the lab. Kate slumped back to her desk. Picked up the phone and dialed Jamison's number.

Are phone cords **designed** *to tie themselves into knots? Basic law of physics, or something?*

After five rings, she went to his answering machine. "Larry, this is Kate Miller. Sorry I missed you. I'd like to show you my Chinatown story before it goes to press. So if you could come by tomorrow morning, that would be great."

She hung up and called Travis's house.

"Hi Brian. Is your dad home yet?"

"Hey, Kate. Uh, nope."

"Oh, have you heard from him?"

"Nope."

"That's strange. Would you like some company?"

"Sure, if you bring ice cream." She sensed this sharp kid was *working the room.*

"Yeah, as long as you can stomach double chocolate."

At that, his voice perked up. "Nice. You bet."

29

NEXT MORNING, JAMISON PARKED AT A DIAGONAL CURBSIDE and hiked toward the front entrance of the Courier newspaper building. He spotted Kate at her desk, typing away, paying more attention to her screen than her keyboard. Their eyes connected. She obviously recognized his uniform.

She looked worried but still managed to hoist a smile. She said, "Morning... Larry. Any contact with Sam?"

He offered his most casual shrug. "No, but it's okay. He's a pro. Count on it. Try not to worry."

SHE WASN'T BUYING IT. "DON'T GIVE ME THAT. YOU SEEM more worried than me."

"There you go, assuming the worst. C'mon, let's have some positive thinking around here. You can start by telling me what you learned in Chinatown."

She welcomed the change of pace. "Plenty. Look...."

She brought their attention to her computer screen. Jamison bent forward to read over her shoulder. He then glanced down at a photo lying right next to the keyboard.

Lu Chang smiled from behind his counter. On the far right, a profiled figure. He was reaching for an item on the shelf *behind the counter*.

Kate heard Jamison's sharp intake of a small breath. She turned to see his eyes were round and his eyebrows burrowed into his forehead. Something surprised him.

Kate said, "What's up?"

"Nothing, Kate."

He bent forward again and peered at the screen while Kate stared at him.

Nothing, indeed. This guy may be a good cop, but a lousy liar.

Outside his camp that night, Travis walked side-by-side with Hudson. Behind them, three bear carcasses hung from a tree in fading light.

Hudson said, "Nice animals, Baker. What time will you be back?"

Travis tried to look like he couldn't wait to get back out there. "Should be there right after supper. Gotta check the station."

"Remember, no games, no company, and no surprises."

"Relax, Hudson. You worry too much."

They stopped walking. Looked directly at one another.

Hudson said, "Maybe you don't worry enough, Baker."

Travis considered making another smart-ass remark, but just shrugged and said, "See you tomorrow."

He tossed Sackett and Hudson a wave, climbed into his pickup, and drove away.

30

THE PICKUP SPRAYED SOME SMALL STONES AS TRAVIS slewed up the long gravel driveway. He'd been away from home too long. Even his "new" truck seemed to sense that.

His headlights lit up a fawn standing near the stairs. As Travis closed the truck door, the fawn approached him and sniffed, looking for a handout.

Travis stooped and nuzzled the small deer with huge brown eyes while he held the little fella's ears in his hands with affection.

"Nice to see you too, little guy."

Travis hiked up the stairs and padded into the house.

The tinkle of Kate and Brian washing and drying

dishes in the kitchen carried to the front door as he closed it behind him to announce his presence. Nothing worse than sneaking up on someone, unless....

Brian came running. "Dad! You're home! You missed a great supper."

"Hi son. Any leftovers?"

Travis sidled up to Kate. "Hi, gorgeous."

Kate tried to look both relieved and annoyed. She failed and smiled. Relief won. "Nice of you to come home."

"Nice of you to be here when I do."

He wrapped his arms around Kate after she removed her glasses and kissed her full on the lips. Brian tried not to watch.

"I could get used to this."

"Well, Mr. Warden, sir, you possess the power. Don't you?"

Brian ran into the kitchen to fetch the plate of leftovers out of the fridge.

Officer Sam Travis shoveled down some leftover corned-beef hash and a pile of green beans while Kate fussed over some dishes, glasses, and silverware. He *hated* green beans, especially with hash, or with anything else, for that matter. But Kate was kind enough to drum up the chow.

Five minutes later, he loosened his belt a

notch and they headed for the living room together.

A PAIR OF DRY OAK LOGS CRACKLED IN THE FIREPLACE. Brian was reading a magazine on the floor. Kate and Travis plopped onto the couch.

Travis said, "I gotta to tell you something important." He waited until he was sure he had their full attention.

"I don't want to alarm you, but you should pay close attention around here for anyone or anything suspicious. The men I'm involved with in this case are dangerous and unpredictable.

"If either of you see or hear something unusual, I want you to call the State Police and Larry Jamison right away. They've been briefed and will come running if you call."

Brian got up off the floor to sit on the arm of the couch next to his dad. "We'll be okay. We're worried about *you*."

Sam smiled. "I'm fine, and I'm being very careful. I want you to be, too. Okay? Time for bed, son. I'll see you off in the morning."

"Night, Dad. And Kate, thanks for coming over, I guess. Thanks for the ice cream, too."

Kate smiled and then reached across Sam's lap

to squeeze the boy's arm. "Brian, you can always call."

He cast his eyes down and waggled his head up and down. Stood to approach Kate. Pecked her on the cheek—the bashful brush of a gentle feather. As he scurried off to bed, Kate and Travis smiled at the gesture and snuggled a little closer together.

TRAVIS STROKED KATE'S HAIR. WITH HIS EYES CLOSED, HE laid his head on top of hers, he said, "Thanks for keeping close to him while I'm working on this. He didn't mind you sleeping here?"

"Nope. He's still a little boy. And we talked a lot about things that were troubling him. It's easier to get to know him when you're not around."

Travis wasn't sure why that tickled his uneasiness muscle, but it didn't matter. The two of them getting along—that mattered.

Kate rolled her eyes to her happy place as Sam stroked her hair. She nestled her head farther up onto his chest, underneath his chin.

She purred, "I met Captain Jamison yesterday after I completed my story about the Chinese connection. There's a copy for you on your desk."

"Find out anything interesting?"

"Medicinal purposes, mostly, but a few items are scary expensive—the true aphrodisiacs."

"How about sources or export information?"

Kate seemed embarrassed that she didn't have more to offer. "Nothing. Very close-mouthed about that."

"Not surprising. I hope to have more on that myself. I'll read it tomorrow morning before I leave."

Kate jerked her head up to catch his eye. "So soon?"

"Yeah. They're expecting me."

She sensed a slight quiver in his hand as he stroked her hair. He was as tense as her senior editor. "So, how much danger are we all in, Sam?"

"I'm just being cautious. My cover is good, and there is nothing to link me to you or Brian."

"Gosh, that sure makes me feel better." The sarcasm in her voice was unmistakable. But then she grew dead serious. "Please be careful."

"Sorry, Kate. I never intended to have my work affect you in any way. Wouldn't you rather be with someone who keeps regular hours, or who doesn't run out as soon as the phone rings?"

Kate touched one finger to his lips. Then she kissed them.

She said, "Goes both ways, babe. Got my name

plastered to a tell-all article on this *Chinese connection.* Let's wrestle over this in bed, okay?"

He grinned, but was still thinking hard. "When I get through with this, I'd like to make this permanent."

The fire crackled.

31

THE NEXT MORNING. TRAVIS STOOD IN THE KITCHEN AT the extreme limit of the wall phone's spiral cord, knotted, of course.

"Hudson, Charles M., Sackett, Randall, no middle initial, McRae, Anthony R.

"Larry, just run 'em and when I'm able to get back to you, let me know what you've learned. I have to leave by early afternoon and pick up some supplies to get back by nightfall... Don't worry.... Okay."

Kate entered the kitchen dressed for work.

"Wow! You always look this good in the morning?"

Kate grinned big. "Sex fiend! I have to go. And please—"

"Yeah, I know. I will. Keep an eye on Brian."

She kissed Travis, hustled through the living room, and out the front door.

32

NIGHT HAD FALLEN. TRAVIS TRUNDLED INTO THE poacher's camp carrying a large knapsack. He noticed Sackett was busy whittling again, putting a sharp point on another stick. McRae carried firewood and was walking much easier. Hudson stood with his back to Travis, taking a long pull from a bottle of vodka.

Travis said, "Brought you guys some treats." He threw a trio of sandwiches to McRae, several bags of candy to Sackett, and a bottle to Hudson.

Hudson said, "Glad to see you made it back, Baker boy."

"How'd you guys do today?"

McRae divvied up the sandwiches. "Got two nice ones. Let's eat. I'm starving."

––––––––––––

A GREAT HORNED OWL SWOOPED FROM A TREE AND captured a mouse. It landed with a whisper and a light touch on a tree limb that sagged under her weight. Silenced the mouse—ended its panic by snapping its neck in her powerful beak.

With a quick lunge into a nearby meadow's tall grass, a coyote captured a rabbit in its powerful jaws and trotted off.

From within the shadows of dense underbrush, a spider enveloped and killed a moth in its web.

The cycle of life.

––––––––––––

THE FOUR MEN ALL HEARD A FEW OF THESE SOUNDS, BUT saw none of it. Travis understood.

You just need to know what you're listening to.

They all grew lethargic. After almost an hour of sitting, eating, drinking and listening, Hudson said, "You fuckers ought to turn in. We got a big day ahead of us tomorrow."

The forest grew still as a mass grave. The campfire flickered low, its embers glowing, now covered with ash.

An hour later, a pair of boots made their way toward Hudson's and Travis's tent. A hand unzipped the doorway. The boots entered the tent. Startled Travis awake. A heavy sap struck his left temple with a dull *thud*.

Next thing Travis knew, they had tied him from behind and around his waist. The force on his shoulder sockets from hanging by his bound wrists and elbows convinced him he needed to lose ten pounds—if he didn't die before dawn.

He wore only his underwear, because that's how he slept, and his feet were bound—way too tight for decent circulation, or for struggling to stay afloat.

They now suspended him three feet off the ground by a block and tackle. The near-freezing temps prickled his skin like thousands of needles. Morning's pre-twilight glow meant he'd been hanging there for a while. Unconscious. And damn-near naked.

Shit!

As he made sense of what had happened, he grunted through his clamped jaw, "What are you crazy bastards doing?"

. . .

SACKETT'S ENORMOUS FIST PUMMELED TRAVIS'S STOMACH. He wretched. Hudson nodded to McRae, who released the line around Travis's waist with a quick slash from his brand new BenchMade knife. Travis swung out over the icy lake water. Before the arc of his swinging diminished, they plunged him into the inky depths.

Bubbles exploded around him. His eyes shot wide with sparks. And more needles. Shock waves surged through him at the unexpected and violent turn of events.

The near-freezing water was already drawing blood away from his vital organs to keep his extremities viable. He'd be dead in minutes. Even though it was futile, he struggled so hard against the ropes that his small muscles were already tearing in his back and sides.

Then, the remote possibility of life returned.

HUDSON NODDED. MCRAE AND SACKETT HOISTED TRAVIS up from the lake, leaving him suspended six feet over the water. The block and tackle squeaked like an ancient grocery cart wheel with the load of a one-hundred-ninety-five-pound body.

Travis gasped and spit and coughed and shook the water out of his eyes.

Hudson spit out the words. "So, maybe you're a warden. Huh, hotshot?"

"You assholes! I'm no fuckin' warden!" The words came out a seething stutter. His jaw chattered, and his skin had turned a bluish-white in the beams of their powerful lantern-battery flashlights.

Hudson smiled. Then nodded to Sackett and McRae. Once more, Travis was plunged into the water. They kept him submerged longer this time. After almost a minute, McRae and Sackett tugged on the rope leading down from the tree limb that overhung the lake. The block and tackle creaked and squeaked again under the strain.

As Travis's head reemerged, his hoarse gasp and softer sputtering signaled he'd come close to drowning.

"We ran your truck numbers, Baker, or whoever you are, and guess what? It came back to a government motor pool. You could die tonight without a mark on you, other than a few rope burns."

TRAVIS SHOOK SO HARD IT CAUSED HIM TO START SWINGING erratically. Needles stabbed into every inch of his skin. Now, it felt like they were barbed and someone was jerking them out—all at once.

Those stabs hurt the worst where ropes binding his ankles pinched off the flow of blood to his feet, but especially just above his now-numb hands. The absolute worst, though, was when he hit the water again and there was no feeling at all in his torso. Like it was already a corpse but connected to a head with a half-alive brain.

Despite all that was happening, he thought of Brian and Kate with icy clarity. They'd wonder what happened to him. How his job got him killed—like Murdock. If he survived this, he'd get the assholes who guaranteed that truck was clean.

Travis chattered, "You're all crazy! Let me explain!"

Down again into the water so cold there were floating crystals that still survived three plunges of almost-dead meat stirring up their otherwise serene surface. Longer yet. Up again. How long....? Now Travis gasped and coughed up at least a quart of the pure water that was killing him more with each passing second.

"You won't last too much longer, Baker boy. Better talk fast!"

He almost failed to get the words out. Took some time. His jaw convulsed and cramped. Struggled to get any sound past his teeth. They were banging into each other like little jackhammers.

He said, "I... bought it... at the annual... government auction. I got the papers. I can prove—"

Hudson nodded, and they plunged Travis back into the water by letting go of the rope and watched it waggle, eager to shed its load.

Sackett said, "What d'ya think, boss? We can check."

Hudson said, "No balls to kill one more, Randy?"

"Charlie, we can always off him after we get our money. And besides, we need the help.

Hudson thought about that. "You might be right. We'll use him for now. But there's something about him...."

Hudson nodded, and they hauled Travis up and out of the water. Unconscious and hypothermic, they thought they might have already lost him. They checked his pulse. Weak, but regular.

Hudson looked at McRae. "Leave him tied, but put him in a bag next to the fire. Throw his ass into my tent after an hour. We'll patch things up in the morning."

33

THE SUN HAD ALREADY PEEKED OVER THE TREES ON THE far side of the glassy lake half an hour earlier. It was a chilly morning.

Travis woke up inside a tent thinking a Mack truck had flattened him. He wondered if frostbite had eaten any fingers or toes that were still buried inside the smelly old sleeping bag zipped up tight around him.

When he realized he was still bound, hand and foot, he growled and sneered and his eyes flashed around. Spotted Hudson staring at him.

"Relax, Baker. Bet you'd like to get hold of me, huh? For now, you're alive. Be thankful for that."

"You bastard. I'm no warden. Check all my papers. You seem to have a way of doing that, but you're drawing fucked-up conclusions."

Hudson said, "I'm alive today because I trust what my instincts tell me about a man, and let's just say I don't get a warm fuzzy about you."

Contrary to his words, Hudson reached over, unzipped the bag that kept Travis alive in not much more than his birthday suit, flicked open a serrated blade, and cut his bonds.

Travis sat up, rubbed his wrists, and lunged for Hudson. He managed a solid punch to Hudson's groin before Sackett crawled into the tent. He pulled Travis outside like he was an almost-pink-again rag doll, still in just his once-white boxers.

Sackett chuckled. "Easy fella. Just had to play all the angles. So settle down and I won't have to hurt ya."

HUDSON CRAWLED OUT OF THE TENT BEHIND THEM. McRae emerged out of the other tent at the ruckus. Still massaging his crotch, Hudson growled, "We're behind schedule. We'll split up into two teams. Me and Baker and you two. Don't feed the dogs till we get back."

To Travis, he said, "No gun for you, Baker boy."

Rubbing his wrists and glaring at Hudson, Travis said, "You take five seconds to re-load that damn crossbow. If a bear knocks your ass down, I'll be damn sure to throw a big fuckin' rock at him."

Hudson paused, looked at Travis. "Always got an answer, don'tcha?" Five seconds of silence later, "Okay, Baker. But I'll be behind you, watching. I still got my magnum."

"Whatever. I'll remember that. Now you mind if I get dressed? Freezin' my ass off over here."

BOOTS CRUNCHED DRIED LEAVES UNDERFOOT AS TRAVIS hustled up a wooded trail, with Hudson close behind, his crossbow cocked and at the ready. Travis suspected the bastard had it aimed between his own shoulder blades. No pressure, though.

Ten minutes later, the hounds were baying at a fever pitch, following a hot bear track as a large beech tree rose in front of them, filling their field of vision.

A small cub clung in desperation to a sizable limb in that tree. The little guy looked down at the half-dozen dogs barking and howling and yipping. Whites in the cub's ebony eyes flashed with fear.

Hudson howled louder than the dogs. "Sweet meat in a tree! Yeah! Baker, tie off them dogs! This baby's mine!"

He aimed, lit up the cub with his laser spot and fired.

Clack-whoosh!

Struck him through the forearm. The cub screamed. Hudson reloaded and fired another bolt into his flesh. The baby bear's searing bleat sounded non-stop, now. HIs mother also howled in a blood-lust rage.

"Boy, these little bastards can take a shot, can't they?" Travis listened to the keening of the cub and the chortling of the bastard firing steel rods into the baby bear's flesh.

Out of the brush, six-hundred pounds of pissed-off mama bear charged Hudson. Knocked him on his back like he was a sapling that stood between her and her baby. She clawed at his heavy clothing, aiming her powerful jaws for his neck. The only thing between him and mama bear's vengeance was the hardened spring steel of his crossbow. Now *he* screamed. "Kill her! Shoot her! Kill the bitch!"

Travis was on the bear's side. But he realized he must act. He wrestled Hudson's forty-one magnum from his holster and fired a round into the base of the bear's skull. The sow let out a low moan as she relinquished her last vestige of life.

Hudson rolled the huge sow off —almost an impossible task—with no help from Travis. Blood from the bear and Hudson's wounds covered his clothing and his face.

Spitting the bear's blood from his mouth, Hudson grabbed the stock of his crossbow that was still cocked and locked. In a cruel rage, he fired a third killing shot into the cub that landed next to his mother.

The dogs fell silent. Travis spotted a wide scar across the she-bear's nose, recognizing her from the earlier tranquil scene when she and her cubs foraged together in peace—just before he downed McRae with his trip wire.

Scarface.

He tried to suppress sadness and anger, but failed.

Travis spit on the dried leaves at his feet and sneered at Hudson. "I should've let her rip you to pieces after last night." Nobody said anything as everybody was huffing in shock and exhaustion.

"Do you still think I'm a warden?"

Hudson attended to his wounds while he worked. But he never looked away from "Baker."

"Fuckin' devils! Now let's get these animals done up."

THAT EVENING, A DOUBLE ROW OF DEAD BEARS HUNG FROM a game pole. The four men slouched around a rip-roaring fire. All were exhausted from dressing and field processing the day's kills.

Hudson grinned with his bruised face from the almost lethal encounter with *Scarface*. He said, "That makes ten. We gotta move 'em—tonight."

Clearly, Charlie moved slower with what looked like pain from bruised ribs and stiffness from bandages Sackett had wrapped around both of his arms. He wore his still-shredded camo jacket over them. Serves him right. Probably now thought of that ripped-up jacket as a badge of courage.

Travis needed to know. "Where do I fit in?"

Hudson got up—slowly. That was the cue for the others to move, too. "Let's get these loaded. Baker, you drive the other truck. We have 'em hidden down the trail."

"Where we takin' 'em?"

"No more fuckin' questions. We'll stay at the 920 Motel in Rogue River. I'll make the arrangements from there."

34

THE MOTEL COULDN'T HAVE BEEN SEEDIER. AT LEAST IT adjoined a restaurant and bar with a dance floor.

Inside the room they all shared, Travis peeked through the cheap drapes, like he was on watch so as not to draw attention to himself. Spotted Hudson making a phone call from a phone booth outside—not his room phone. Smart.

Hudson shuffled back into the room. A frigid blast followed him in, along with a few flurries. A storm was coming. "All set for tonight. Seven o'clock. Usual place."

Travis shrugged and said, "What do I have to do?"

"Do as you're told and nothing more. I'll handle all the bartering."

"What do you figure this is worth?"

Sackett saw no harm showing off for Travis. "Figuring this time of year and the quality of the galls... should be around forty or fifty thou'."

Travis said, "Split four ways?"

McRae snickered and glanced sideways at Travis while he paid most of his attention to ripping away the plastic wrapper from a strip of beef jerky. "Why's that? You don't contribute nothin' to the dogs."

Through his customary cold-eyed squint that now caused him some discomfort from the swelling, Hudson said, "Stop pushin', Baker boy."

"Uh-huh. How much was saving your ass worth?"

"I told you to stop pushin'!"

To emphasize his point, and maybe draw a little blood, Hudson lunged toward Travis with his big-ass hide-stripping knife.

Travis side-stepped the blade and locked Hudson's elbow under his forearm, almost breaking it. Hudson winced and yelped. The knife clattered to the dirty linoleum floor. Travis spun Hudson around and immobilized him with his left hand gripping his lower jaw and his other arm around the nasty man's little neck. Sackett took a step quick toward Travis.

"Easy boys. Three more pounds of pressure and he's dead. All it takes to snap his neck."

Hudson croaked, "Back off!" They did. Travis released Hudson and smiled.

Travis said, "What say let's all behave and get this over and done with, okay?"

35

THE DAY WAS ONLY MINUTES OLD, JUST PAST MIDNIGHT. A yellow light atop a crooked pole illuminated the painted wall. The sign on top of the large warehouse's people door in one-foot letters said:

Wong Importers, Inc.

The same name was ten feet tall in faded paint on the alley side of the otherwise well-maintained three-story brick building.

The adjacent loading dock on the alley side had

a sliding bar gate with razor wire on top. At least one remote camera with its blinking red-diode light within the razor wire enclosure was aimed outward.

Hudson said, "Just wait here. You'll be told what to do."

Travis was both nervous and excited. This was the next rung on the ladder. "Oh, I'm sure about that, Chucky boy." Hudson didn't hear him mutter this under his breath.

Hudson walked up to the door, rang a soundless bell and waited. A half minute passed. Then, they saw Hudson engaged in a brief conversation with a small speaker in a box to the left side of the door. He walked back to the truck. He spoke loud enough so the men in both trucks understood his orders.

"Okay, unload 'em on the dock, fast. I'm going inside." He waved them to their right where the gate opened. They drove the trucks in. The gate closed behind them.

They backed both trucks up to the loading dock. Sackett and McRae unloaded their truck.

TRAVIS NEEDED TO MAKE SOMETHING HAPPEN. HE STOOD at the rear of his truck, slid the key into its slot for the bed cap's swing-up door and snapped it off in the lock.

Sackett and McRae were less than ten feet away. Travis said, "Shit! You guys got an extra key for this?"

Sackett looked over, frowning. "What's wrong?"

"The damn key broke off in the lock. I'll find Charlie and see if he has one."

"You can't—"

Travis was already at the door toward the front of the building from the alley-side dock, ringing the silent bell. The door slid open about two feet and two large Oriental men appeared in the slot, led Travis inside and closed the door behind him.

Travis hollered, "Hudson-san. Hudson-san!"

He held up the broken key. One goon nodded recognition and guided him through the warehouse with the second goon close behind.

Travis saw several walk-in coolers. Through the windows in their insulated doors, it was obvious they were full of protected but very dead animals: bear, cougar, elk, deer, and waterfowl—all in various stages of processing. The volume and variety staggered him.

His rear guard shouted at him in, what? Chinese? Korean? The lead guard turned around at the disturbance, and was clearly pissed about Travis playing tourist.

They hustled him to a corridor with two more

Asian men standing guard. His rear guard spoke in a staccato cadence to one of the burly men and left.

Trying to sound conversational, Travis smiled and said, "Nice evening, huh? Think it'll snow? You're an asshole, you know."

Nope. No speaky English.

The other guard entered and then re-emerged from the locked room ten seconds later. He motioned for Travis to enter. Behind a large black desk sat a well-dressed young Asian female.

She sat on a backless chair. And yet her back was ramrod straight, as if she had a stainless rod stuck up her ass. And he was looking at Hudson's back where he perched on the edge of a guest chair facing the Dragon Lady. He looked over his left shoulder and up at Travis.

"How did you get in here, Baker?"

"I walked in with my Boy Scout friend here," as he offered a smile and a nod at his lead guard next to him.

He looked at the woman. "Nice place you have here, ma'am." Must be Madam Wong—Dragon Lady.

Hudson tried but failed to conceal his anger. He seethed, "What do you want?"

Travis tried on his most innocent expression. "I need an extra key for the truck cap. You know, the topper." He held up the key stub. "This cheap one broke."

Now, Hudson leaned toward Travis and motioned him to stoop down so he could whisper through clenched teeth without moving his lips. As if that would prevent the woman four feet away from hearing him. "Jimmy the fuckin' thing! I ain't got no key!"

"Okay, don't get excited. I'll handle it. Sorry if I caused any problem."

TRAVIS WALKED OUT WITH HIS ESCORT. THEY HAD displeased Madam Wong. One look at her Botox'd face that was so tight it precluded any meaningful expression and he could still see she was pissed, but wanted their product.

He heard Hudson say, "My apologies, Ms. Wong. A new man who will kill many bears for you."

Outside, they finished offloading the bears that were then trundled in from the dock by several of the warehouse workers on wheeled carts. Hudson came out ten minutes later and climbed into the truck with Travis.

"How'd that key break, Baker?"

"I just turned the thing, and it came apart. I

couldn't unload them through the windows, could I?"

"Well, whatever. It's done. We did good. Get us back to the motel."

Hudson fiddled with the radio while Travis drove. An hour later, they passed a sign:

East Salisbury Cemetery.

36

BACK IN THE MOTEL ROOM ANOTHER HOUR LATER, HUDSON slumped at the cheap table that made a rickety elbow rest. Sackett slouched in the only other chair. McRae stood six feet away, leaning against the grungy wallpapered wall, while Travis stretched out on one of the two single beds. It was two-thirty in the morning.

Glasses with ice and two half-empty bottles of hard liquor stood guard on the windowsill next to the door.

The prospect of a payday fueled the glint in McRae's eyes. "How much we get, Charlie?"

Hudson was stacking bills. He said with a grin,

"Forty-three thousand, five-hundred. Here are your shares."

He handed out small piles of large bills. "Ten grand for you and Randy. Half that for Baker."

As each man counted their share and put the bills in their individual wallets or pockets, Hudson said, "Any complaints?"

Travis smirked, stuffed his share in the hip pocket of his jeans, and shuffled out of the room with McRae close behind.

McRae said, "Let's party! Meet you losers at the bar!"

Hudson looked up from leafing through his cash to catch Sackett's eye. The two other men had already stepped outside and closed the door behind them.

"You keep your eye on him. I figure you and Tony will be splitting his share before the night's over."

"Gotcha, boss."

37

920 MOTEL BAR

Rogue River, Massachusetts

THE ALL-NIGHT HONKY-TONK BAR WAS DIM, LOUD, AND smokey. Middle-aged truckers and rednecks in flannel shirts, blue jeans sporting big silver belt buckles and cowboy boots laughed and reeked of stale beer and cheap cigarettes.

A few women in tight pants or low-cut dresses wore too much makeup and too many hard miles. But most looked good enough by last call.

The marquee boasted the band *Easy Lovin'* was returning for an encore presentation that night.

Hudson, Sackett, McRae and Travis all sat

together, waiting to order their meal. Sackett and McRae had already filled the small round table with at least twenty beer bottles. Their attractive server tried to clear the tables. But Sackett hollered at her and grabbed her wrist. Hard.

She winced and said, "Just tryin' to tidy up your table, mister. Let go!"

"You dumb bitch. That's how we keep score. Don't you know nothin'?"

His slurred speech also kept score for everyone around him. McRae laughed—more of a snort—and slapped the girl's ass so hard it had to sting.

She jerked away from Sackett, who had already lost interest in her for his half-full beer. She wheeled around and slapped McRae's face hard enough to jerk his head to the side, causing him to tear up. That pissed him off enough to bunch up his right fist and slug the girl in the gut. Didn't want to mark up that pretty face. He probably thought he might still have a chance with her if she'd see the error of her ways.

The bartender came over to haul her away before some of his regulars took matters into their own hands. Just that those boys were buyin' a *lot* of beers and they were tipping big. He slipped a twenty into her hand. She understood. She needed this job.

The juke box played non-stop country tunes

loud enough for passing cars outside to hear—even if their windows weren't open.

The boys ate triple-stack burgers, fries and ordered dessert. The special was a Kit-Kat wafer stabbed into a scoop of soft-serve vanilla ice cream and drowned in a homemade chocolate and whiskey sauce.

<hr />

TRAVIS ROSE FROM HIS PADDED VINYL CHAIR WITH A DIRTY chunk of duct tape covering a jagged tear near the center of its red seat. He needed to get away from that woman-beating McRae before he beat the asshole bloody himself.

"Gotta hit the head."

He met a couple of biker-looking dudes coming out of the men's room, holding hands.

Seriously?

While standing at the urinal, he checked out a vending machine bolted to the wall at shoulder level on the wall to his right: prophylactics, after-shave, mouthwash and Ex-Lax.

All the essentials for a night on the town, eh, boys?

Travis smiled. After taking care of business, he dropped four quarters in the machine's slot and twisted the rightmost knob. A plastic-wrapped twin pack of Ex-Lax dropped into the grab tray.

He walked back into the countrified cacophony floating in drama-saturated smoke and sloughed back to the table.

Hudson was at the bar talking to the waitress with the tight ass McRae had slugged. She smelled cash—a real trooper. McRae and Sackett were each dancing with a couple of locals.

A DIFFERENT WAITRESS ARRIVED AT THE TABLE WITH TWO desserts. She flashed her false lashes at Travis. "Two house specials, handsome."

As she bent too far over the table, exposing ample cleavage, she purred, "You see anything else you might like, darlin'?"

"No, thanks, Ma'am. You sure have great-looking desserts here."

In a husky whisper she said, "Wanna sample the private stuff?"

"I reckon my wife might raise the dickens if I did."

She grinned with sad eyes as she sauntered away, muttering back at him over her shoulder. "Too bad, sugar. Seems all the good ones are spoken for these days."

. . .

TRAVIS LOOKED AROUND. THE BOYS WERE OVER THERE thinking with their little heads, not looking his way. He pulled the chocolate Kit Kat bar from Sackett's and McRae's desserts, and gobbled them down. He'd grunt out an extra hundred push-ups tomorrow. Substituted the Ex-Lax.

Five minutes later, the music stopped. Hudson strolled back to the table. Not in a straight line. Then, the next song started. The other two jokers were still hanging onto a couple of gals like they would never let go.

While stirring the rum and diet he was nursing, Travis asked, "So, besides killing things, what else do you do, Charlie?"

"More questions, huh?"

"Just making small talk. What makes a man like you a poacher? The money's good, but not enough to live the good life."

Hudson scratched the stubble on his chin with the tips of all the fingers of his left hand. "Why? Because I like triggers, I guess. I like the triggers on rifles, shotguns, pistols, and crossbows, anything that can kill from a distance."

Then, as if the devil himself was pulling trip wires downward on the corners of his mouth, he growled, bared his teeth, just a little, and flexed all ten fingers like they all itched for action.

"Because *I* get to decide which ones live and which ones die. I pull the trigger and the power of life and death is *all mine*. I'd love to do it to people if I knew I wouldn't be caged for life. If the Devil ever needed a hit man, I'd fuckin' volunteer with pleasure. Answer your question, Baker boy?"

He laughed, but it came out more like a screech from that movie, *The Exorcist*.

On the outside, Travis snickered. Inside, though, he shivered.

This here is one evil little fucker.

"Yeah, thanks for sharing that with me. I'm understanding you better now, Charlie."

Flashes of Frank's blank face intertwined with Hudson cackling as he killed those bear cubs and their mama. Travis smiled at Hudson.

Gonna get you, ya son of a bitch.

AFTER THE SONG ENDED, THE TWO GALS WHO WERE foolish enough to mix it up with McRae and Sackett scurried for the safety of the women's restroom. The boys stumbled back to the table and plopped down in their chairs. Their ice cream was half-melted. They inhaled their desserts.

Travis found it hard to understand Sackett's slurring mumble. Ice cream dripped into his black whiskers. "No sweets for you, Baker?"

"Nah, it's enough just watchin' you eat yours, Randy."

All three of the poachers wandered up to the bar again to chat up some new gals. Some never see past the twenties and fifties....

38

AFTER MORE DANCES WITH MORE GALS, HUDSON returned to the table again, bored.

Through the smoke and noise, Travis caught the sudden pained expression on Sackett's face on the far side of the dance floor, close to the bar. Travis grinned and shook his head, just a little, in a "serves-you-right" expression. Sackett left the perplexed woman on the dance floor with a mad dash for the men's room. Travis continued to nurse his rum and diet.

He caught Hudson staring at him. "You look happy all of a sudden."

Travis shrugged, nodded toward the woman Sackett had just abandoned. "Just watching

Randy and his moves. Think I'll get a refill at the bar."

AS HE APPROACHED THE BAR, TRAVIS EYED THE PAY PHONE in the hall next to the men's room door. With a furtive look over his right shoulder, he made sure neither Hudson nor McRae were watching. Detoured toward that phone as if he were headed down the blind hall to take a leak.

He removed the handset from its hook. Pulled a dime out of his pocket. Inserted it into the slot. Waited for the chime to make sure the phone had taken his money. He dialed Jamison's number. One ring. Another ring. Three rings....

C'mon, Larry, pick up!

"Hello?"

Sackett slammed open the men's room door like he was pissed at it and stumbled out, surprised to see Travis standing there. He hung up and said, "You all right, Randy? You don't look so good."

"Damn! Ah, it's nothin'."

They both returned to the table and Sackett sat down like his ass was made of delicate glass.

Hudson said, "Problem, Randy?"

"Ohhh, boy. I swear someone stretched my asshole over a fifty-five-gallon oil drum."

Travis dropped into his chair. Corners of the duct tape patch stuck to his jeans. He said, "Musta been somethin' you ate. Gotta recycle some of this beer, myself."

BAKER HEADED FOR THE MEN'S ROOM AGAIN. SACKETT wasn't far behind.

While standing at the trough, a man to Baker's right glanced over at him. Sackett entered a stall behind them unseen. His "stomach" was screaming at him, and he wasn't proud of it.

That's when he heard the man next to Baker say, "Hey! I know you! You're that EPO . You got those guys we turned in a couple years ago in South County for jackin' them deer."

Then he heard Baker mumble, "You must be mistaken, mister. I'm no friggin' EPO."

"Never forget a face, man. Uh, Tagiss, Trevis, Travis! That's it. Travis."

"Wrong guy, partner. You've had too much to drink."

Sackett noticed Baker's' boots as he walked past his stall. A malicious sneer sculpted his face.

Travis, huh? Charlie was right!

Sackett reached over for the waistline of his

camo pants and canvas belt down around his ankles as he stood up in a hurry. He zipped and buckled. Then, with a groan and a frown, unbuckled and unzipped again. His pants dropped back down around his ankles as he issued another low moan and dropped back down.

Travis stood outside the bar, getting some fresh air.

Second-hand smoke's gonna take me yet.

He took a few deep breaths and craned his neck to gaze at the clear, starlit sky. He thought for a moment, looked back inside through the windows under the joint's covered porch, took the truck keys out of his pocket. His mind was made up.

After unlocking the truck, he crawled into the driver's seat, turned her over, and peeled out. The dash lights illuminated his grim expression. After driving for a while, he took a right at a sign that read,

East Salisbury
Cemetery
1 Mile

THE RUSTY WROUGHT-IRON ARCH OVER THE GRAVEYARD'S entrance felt like a bad omen. Turned off the lights and got out of the truck. The door creaked when he closed it. Another omen?

The entire scene felt creepy, but he had to do this. Walked by several headstones. He stopped at one and knelt. He ran his fingers into the recesses of stone that spelled his dead wife's name.

Said nothing.

39

AT THEIR TABLE BY THE DANCE FLOOR IN THE 920 Motel's bar, Sackett chattered with Hudson and McRae. Hudson marched up to the bar, barked something at the bartender, who frowned at his rudeness, but reached under the bar, handed him a phone book. Hudson fingered through a few pages and then his face flashed recognition.

He marched back to the table where he'd left the two men and said, "Get off your asses. We're goin' huntin' again."

The gleam in his eye surprised even the two hardened poachers who sat there looking up at their fearless leader blank-faced.

"Well, c'mon, fer crissake!"

The sound of chairs scraping between the band's songs and last gulps of almost-empty beer bottles preceded them hustling out to Hudson's pickup.

All three men rushed out of the bar and drove away. Charlie was all over the road.

BACK AT THE BAR, TRAVIS JUMPED OUT OF HIS TRUCK AND noticed Hudson's was gone. He headed back inside. Four strangers now sat at "their" table. He spotted the waitress that had mixed it up with McRae earlier.

"Those assholes? Peeled out of here ten minutes ago like their hair was on fire. Looked real excited about somethin'. Good tippers, though."

Travis smiled and thanked her. Slipped her a five. Still standing by the bar, he waved at the bartender, who came over as the waitress hustled off.

"Hey, partner, did you notice where my friends went?"

The burly kid scratched his scraggly beard, and muttered, "Might've." Looked Travis in the eye without blinking while he chomped on a toothpick.

Travis read the kid and grabbed a fifty out of his front jeans pocket. Slid it across the bar.

"Yeah, matter of fact. Funny. The scraggly little one with the mean eyes—no offense—asked for a phone book. Heard him muttering somethin' like 'a fuckin' warden,' or somethin' like that."

A bolt of lightning coursed through Travis. Weakened his knees.

"How long ago?"

"Like I said, maybe ten, fifteen minutes. Hey, mister!"

Travis was already darting for the door at a full run. A few folks turned and stared, but he was already outside, headed for the phone booth just beyond the bar's covered porch. Slammed a dime into the slot and stabbed seven numbers like they were in the center of Charlie Hudson's chest. All he got in return was nobody answering.

"C'mon Brian. Pick up. PICK UP!"

He hung up. His dime rolled down into the little silver return drawer. He snatched it, cycled it back into the slot up top, punched in Jamison's number.

"Larry. No time to explain. Get to my house, fast. State Police, too. I'll meet you. They're heading for my place!"

Travis sprinted to the pickup, slammed it into Drive, and stomped the gas. He spit gravel for twenty feet. The truck screamed in protest. Then, he hit the blacktop. The tires grabbed, chirped, and chattered as the truck's rear-end hopped and bounced up onto the paved two-lane road scattered with the gravel.

His clammy sweat dripped onto the steering wheel as he sped away. Kept asking himself how things could have gone so wrong, so fast. But he knew. That guy in the men's room. The stall door was latched shut. Ex-Lax.

Son-of-a-bitch!

40

Kate sat at the kitchen table. Looked up from scribbling her early thoughts for an article on a notepad and smiled at the sight of Brian through the archway in the living room. He was watching TV.

An unusual sound interrupted her train of thought. She remembered Travis warning them to remain vigilant for anything unusual. She stood and headed for the living room and the front door.

Brian turned his head. "What's the matter, Kate?"

"I don't know. I think I'll put the outside light on."

Kate looked out the window past the porch. Nothing. She headed for the kitchen door at the back of the house to lock it when a skinny stranger with mean eyes appeared in the window. He stood there with his face inches from the glass, just smiling.

Kate gasped and let out a small yelp of alarm. Through the door that she hoped she had locked earlier, she said, "Who are you and what do you want?"

"Name's Walter Drury, ma'am. Sorry to scare you. Lookin' for the EPO."

"What for?"

"I hit a deer with my truck, ma'am. He ran off. But he's wounded real bad. Wonderin' if I couldn't come in and use the phone if my friend Sam ain't here."

Torn with conflict, her indecision paralyzed her. After a full ten seconds, she croaked, "He's not in right now, but I suppose it'd be okay to use the phone."

She doubted the wisdom of her decision even as she unlocked the kitchen door.

HUDSON BURST THROUGH THE DOOR, KNOCKING KATE TO the floor. Sackett and McRae rushed in right behind him.

Kate screamed. It was guttural, primal. "Brian! RUN!"

Hudson hollered to Sackett, "Get the boy!"

He leered down at Kate. "Nice looking. Yep, real nice looking. Bet you're real fun, lady."

Kate scrambled away—toward Brian—on her hands and knees, but Hudson caught her by the ankles after a few feet. He turned her onto her back by twisting her ankles counterclockwise, knocking her head against the cast-iron oven door.

Hudson began lifting and spreading her ankles to draw her in. Kate reached forward. Power-punched him in the groin. He doubled over in the unique pain only a man would understand. But he refused to release his vice-like grasp on her left forearm.

AS SACKETT ENTERED THE ROOM CLUTCHING THE squirming Brian under one massive arm, Hudson jerked Kate off the floor by her arm, her eyes wild with rage—and pain.

Hudson sucked air in between his teeth and lower lip. Sounded like a snake hissing. Clutching his crotch with his left hand and wincing in agony, he said, "I oughta kill you right here in your pretty little kitchen, *bitch!* Instead, maybe I'll let my friends here have some fun with you. I bet you'd like that."

Kate bled from the mouth where her face had hit the stove. She simpered, "Leave the boy alone. I'll do what you say. Just let him go."

Still holding his family jewels, Hudson barely contained his rage. "Nice try. I'm going to leave Mr. Warden a little something to remember me by."

Hudson then drew his knife. Kate's eyes widened, and she shivered under his iron grip.

Brian spotted the knife and screamed, "You leave her alone, you... *bully!*"

41

TRAVIS BORDERED ON LOSING CONTROL OF THE TRUCK, almost careening off the shoulder into the steep ditch—at least six times in as many minutes.

A hub cap spun off the rim and wobbled at an angle down the road behind him. He was mad with panic, swearing to and at himself. He punched the cab's ceiling so hard, it dented the stout steel roof through the headliner.

As he neared his driveway, he killed the lights, skidded to a stop. He tumbled out, leaving the door open. Drew his three-fifty-seven and moved in his quick-sideways-stealth pace up through the brush along the driveway. His finger lay alongside the big pistol's trigger guard, ready for anything... or so he thought.

His pulse quickened further, if that was possible. The house was dark. He painted the air in front of his face with puffs of pale white vapor, like a quarter horse finishing a hard mile. With his back to the porch wall and gun at the ready, he turned the knob, shoved the door open with his left shoulder, and crept quickly inside, his weapon low and ready. Silence. And darkness.

A GUST OF CHILLY WIND OUTSIDE ANNOUNCED THAT nature didn't give a spit what little drama played out inside. Travis entered and moved down the hall toward the bathroom door with his back against the wall. Nothing.

Returning from the bathroom, he wheeled ninety degrees to his right and crouched into a two-handed shooting stance, as if he expected someone to be hiding in the main floor bedroom. The moonlight revealed something wet and shiny that reflected off the floor in the center of the room. His heart pounded against his chest wall.

No!

Travis peered around to either side and stooped to run his index finger through the pool at his feet.

Held it up to the moonbeam shining through the skylight and worked it between his thumb and middle finger.

He stood up fast with his back against the wall once more. Closed his eyes for a second to clear his head. Opened them again and followed the trail. Led through the house to his basement office. The wild pounding of his heart drowned out the stillness all around him. Then....

A small, dark figure hanging from a ceiling joist came into view. With his free hand, Travis reached for the light switch at the base of the stairs without looking and *snicked* it up, even though he feared what he'd see as blood thundered through his temples and the sides of his throat.

The little fawn that always nuzzled him dangled limp from the exposed ceiling joist with its throat cut. Fresh blood still dripped down its neck and pooled on the painted concrete floor beneath him.

SWEARING UNDER HIS BREATH, TRAVIS NOW MOVED through the rest of the house like a careful assassin in a hurry, turning lights on as he cleared each room. He then climbed the stairs, taking three at a time. He shouted, "Brian! Kate! If you're here, talk to me!"

He froze in his tracks and held his breath to listen.

"Brian!"

He entered his son's room. Flicked on the light. Heard a sound from the closet. He approached. Led with his gun low and ready. His hands were shaking, fearing what he'd find.

In an instant, he repositioned into his shooting stance again. Ripped open the closet door so hard, it hit the wall and bounced back to hit his hip. Brought his gun to bear with both hands once more toward its dark interior.

And there was Kate. His heart ripped apart.

Her face was swollen and covered with blood with a gag stuffed in her mouth. She shook her head side-to-side in undisguised rage and fear. Then she saw it was Travis. She dropped her chin to her chest in exhaustion. Issued a ragged moan of relief through her half-clotted nostrils. They'd tied her ankles, and her torn blouse exposed most of her left breast.

Even though he was not yet sure if a threat still existed, he holstered his big revolver, knelt, and pulled the gag out of Kate's mouth. While he untied her, he croaked like a panicky bullfrog, "Are you alright? What did they do to you? Where's Brian?"

Now that she could speak, she only had enough

breath to sob in earnest. Between shaky inhales and a voice pock-marked with shuttered cries, she said, "Sam, I tried to stop them. They took Brian!"

Just then, Travis heard a stair creak. He held his left index finger to his lips as he retrieved his revolver with his other hand. Kate nodded. She clamped both hands over her bloody lips, winced, but kept her eyes wide open.

Travis took a breath and sprang to his feet. He moved to the door. Thought of how a panther stalked its prey. He was a panther. He'd chew these assholes to shreds. But first, protect and contain.

As he bobbed one eye around the bedroom's door jamb, he glanced down the stairs before he ducked back. He flashed on the figure creeping up the stairs with a weapon leading the way.

He hollered, "Jamison, it's me. I'm with Kate. The house is clear."

"You okay?"

Travis stuck his head out and waved him up as Jamison holstered his revolver.

"Kate needs an ambulance. They've taken Brian. You alone?" His voice quivered as he spoke. This had now become *very* personal. This was no longer just the job.

"State Police should be here any second."

. . .

TRAVIS HURRIED BACK INTO THE BEDROOM AND CROSSED to the closet where Kate still huddled with her hands locked across her lips.

"Kate, honey, it's okay."

Red and blue flashing lights now reflected off the second-floor bedroom ceiling. Travis figured at least two state cruisers must already be in the yard. There'd be two troopers in each. A lot of firepower.

He took Kate's hands in his own. Helped her up. She was shaking so hard she had trouble standing. Shock. He now wore her blood on his hands and in the cradle of his shoulder where he hugged her.

This. Will. Not. Fucking. Stand....

"Honey, an ambulance is on the way. Larry and I are going after Brian."

Upon hearing Brian's name again, some steely resolved surfaced. Her quivering abated, at least for a moment. She drew Travis in. Pecked him on the cheek, then rubbed some of her own blood away with her thumb that she had left behind. She pushed him away.

"I'm okay. Be careful, but get them, Sam. Bring our Brian back safe."

"We will."

He quick-squeezed her shoulders and turned away. He and Jamison thundered down the stairs, two at a time. Headed for Jamison's official cruiser, and hopped in. Travis slammed the passenger-side door hard enough to make the window rattle.

JAMISON SHOT A LOOK TO HIS RIGHT. HE WAS CONCERNED for his friend. And a little afraid. Said, "where we headed, partner?"

"Their camp first. Then Wong Importers."

Jamison knew bloodlust when he saw it. He was looking at it right at that very scary moment.

42

RUTLEDGE GLEN ROAD

JAMISON'S HEADLIGHTS AND A ROW OF ROOFTOP SPOTS illuminated the deserted road with a chilling brilliance. Dust swirled in their wake, now mixed with a few flurries. As they drifted to a stop in a broadside drift, Jamison punched off the headlights.

Travis said, "Let's walk the rest of the way. No lights."

"What about some back-up?"

"You're the backup, Larry. More'd be nice, but the more time they have to set up, the harder it'll be. Even with help. Ready?"

"Let's do it."

Travis and Jamison crept their way up the trail, guns drawn. Nothing but silence and darkness as they approached the poachers' camp. The only light came from a low fire's flickering that threw off crazy gyrating shadows. Travis's hand-signal to Jamison: *approach the camp's perimeter off to his own left.* They were about thirty feet apart as they came into the fire's dim influence.

A WHIMPERING DOG DREW JAMISON'S ATTENTION. A moment later, he heard Travis shout, "Behind you! Hey, McRae!"

Jamison wheeled around just as one poacher charged him with an ax held high. As its head arced toward his head—like decapitation was this guy's intent—Jamison ducked, rolled away, and landed back up on his feet.

AN INSTANT LATER, TRAVIS SAW SACKETT COMING AT HIM, but too late. The ex-pro wrestler landed two heavy blows—one to his stomach and another to the back of his head. Travis went down hard. His gun flew into the brush and disappeared.

"Fuckin' EPO, huh?"

JAMISON DODGED REPEATED SWINGS OF THE AX HELD BY the guy Travis had called McRae. He stumbled backwards into the fire. Sparks and fresh smoke swirled around him.

ON HIS KNEES, TRAVIS SUFFERED ANOTHER CRUSHING blow. Sackett landed a fist to his face—didn't notice which one—knocking him backward. Sackett smiled. Travis tried to get up, but his legs weren't cooperating. Sackett advanced again with delight.

As the wrestler reached to hoist Travis off the ground, Travis kicked Sackett hard in the groin. That stopped his momentum. He staggered backward and bent over, but quickly recovered. Travis tried to retreat.

Sackett's huge hands reached Travis's neck, and lifted him off the ground by his throat with little effort. Sackett smiled, although still affected by that vicious kick to the nuts.

Travis struggled. He repeatedly struck Sackett's

smiling face with both fists. No effect. He was too close to get the force of his elbows in there.

McRae still swung the axe at Jamison. As he ducked under one swing that was so close to his face, he felt the breeze. Jamison advanced and drove the heel of his right palm up into the bridge of McRae's nose with tremendous force, snapping his neck back like a dried twig. Ax=man went down. He would not get up.

He looked over and spotted Travis hanging like a rag doll in the mammoth hands of a guy that reminded him of Hulk Hogan, the pro wrestler turned actor. Looked like Travis was punching the guy's head even while the big bastard was squeezing the life out of his friend.

Jamison pulled himself up and ran to help Travis. He landed two vicious kidney punches to the backside of Hulk Hogan. But they had no effect.

The monster still held Travis by the throat, who was turning a pale blue. This guy's enormous arm swung behind him and backhanded Jamison, a blow with devastating effect. Jamison was back in the dirt.

Though his vision flared with starbursts,

Jamison spotted a twelve-inch stick near the fire. Looked like somebody had whittled it to a point. He grabbed the stick and lunged back toward the big man.

He jumped up onto his back, his left arm wrapped around the monster's tree-trunk throat. He propelled his right arm into a big arc and drove the point of the stick into the hulk's neck, severing his carotid artery. Jamison then jumped down to deliver several rapid-fire blows to the monster's cervical vertebrae.

TRAVIS KNEW THIS COULD BE THE END. EVEN THE ENERGY to take a breath faded. Everything was dimming. He looked into Sackett's crazy eyes, less than two feet away. He could see the fire's flames reflected in those dark eyes. But they grew more distant.

Then, though, Sackett's eyes transformed from an evil flicker to childlike wonder. After that, just blank, like a painter hadn't yet finished them. Everything got warm and wet.

The horizon tilted for both him and Sackett. They transitioned from vertical to horizontal —together.

Once the fireworks behind his closed eyelids died to cinders,
everything...
just...
faded.

43

Fifteen minutes later, both EPOs sat facing the confused fire. Travis had recovered, mostly, and rubbed his bruised throat. Jamison sagged, elbows on knees, slumped over, as if numb all over.

Travis said, "Well, partner, that went pretty well."

Jamison looked at him and snorted. He meant it to be a half-assed chuckle that just went bad.

A voice behind them said, "Thanks for taking those two out."

Both men jumped. Jamison said, "Seriously? How many of these assholes are there, Trav?"

Hudson said, "You think your badges make you so smart?"

Nobody said anything. Then, Hudson added, like he was telling tales out of school, "You've got badges with dirt all over them, right under your fucking noses. You should've let that she-bear take me, Baker, or Officer Travis, or whatever the fuck your name is."

Hudson shuffled into the firelight so the wardens could see him holding a nasty forty-one caliber handgun pointed down at them.

Travis looked up at those mean eyes. "Where's my son?"

"Now, now, let's remain calm. Let's say he's my insurance policy."

"Hudson, I will find you and kill you if you—"

The man *screeched*. "You're in no position to threaten me!"

The vapor from his breath punctuated his malevolent intent. Looked like a bull snorting in defiance at the center of the ring. He spit as he spoke. A snot bubble appeared in the poacher's left nostril and popped as he shouted.

Jamison said, "Give it up, Hudson. You'll just end up like your pals here."

With his free hand, Hudson pointed a flashlight off to his left and behind. In the beam, but surrounded by cold darkness, hung Brian Travis. From the same tree limb over the water. Like two days ago when Travis had almost died from repeated dunking in the icy lake. But with his much smaller body mass, Brian wouldn't last sixty seconds.

Above a gag that covered the lower half of Brian's terrified face, his eyes reflected the fear he saw in his father. He struggled against the rope, even though there was no hope of freeing himself. Like father, like son.

TRAVIS MADE A MOVE TOWARD HUDSON, BUT JAMISON grabbed his arm.

Hudson snarled. "You do have me outnumbered, all right. I'll have to fix that."

The nasty pistol's muzzle flash thrust the night into brilliant confusion as its fire extended two feet beyond the end of its barrel.

Hudson watched in delight, Travis in shock. The bullet had punched Larry in the chest. Jamison toppled like a tree being felled—in slow motion.

"No!" Travis screamed. Sounded like his voice box might never be the same after that guttural shriek.

Travis charged the bright-smiling Hudson about the same time a red dot appeared on the gunman's neck.

Clack-whoosh!

Before Hudson pulled his trigger, and before Travis reached him, a steel bolt pierced Hudson's neck from right to left and a little from behind. As Travis reached Hudson, who had gone stiff, both their expressions registered... surprise. But for very different reasons.

Hudson fell. Travis's momentum helped. And he didn't feel bad about pummeling the asshole as he was dying. Except for the mess.

A FIGURE APPEARED FROM THE DARKNESS OFF TO THEIR left, holding Hudson's crossbow now hanging by his side, no longer cocked and loaded. As the figure approached the fire, a voice said, "Thing shoots a might high."

"Taggart! Thanks for the save, pardner."

As Travis lifted himself off the dead poacher's body, he offered a half-smile of gratitude to the old woodsman and friend of Frank Murdock. He kicked away Hudson's handgun harder than was necessary.

Travis rolled the poacher over. One end of the bolt in his neck dug into the dirt as he did so.

Hudson's blank eyes were stuck open, with small sticks and dried leaves clinging to his pitiful beard. His cold eyes no longer squinted. They were just... vacant.

Travis looked up. It was tricky retrieving his son from that limb as he hung out over the almost frozen water. Travis used a long stick to get him swinging like a pendulum. Once he got his arms tight around Brian's waist, Taggart lowered him by feeding out, hand over hand, the line leading down from the block and tackle on a thick limb where it met the trunk of that old tree.

Travis embraced the most precious thing in his life.

"Dad, I can't breathe."

"Oh, sorry."

He then rushed to his boss and friend to check for a pulse. To his surprise, as he pressed two fingers to Jamison's neck, his eyes popped open. He moaned and croaked as he cleared his throat, "Did we get him?"

"Boss! You're alive!"

"Well, you're sharper than most folks give you credit, Sam." He smiled, but winced in pain. "We get him?"

"Thank Christ you wore your vest, Larry! Yeah, we got him with a little help from an old friend. We gotta get you to a hospital."

"Well, notify the ME 'n get the crime scene techs out here. Got three bodies and a shitload of evidence to secure and catalog."

"Larry, hospital."

AS HE RAISED JAMISON TO A SITTING POSITION, GETTING him ready to hike to where they left the cruiser, Travis asked, "How long were you here, Taggart? Hey, give me a hand?"

They both struggled. Jamison was still mostly dead weight. His nervous system hadn't yet given him permission to resume full mobility, even if the punch in the chest, vest or not, hadn't cracked or broken a few ribs. Travis had seen it before. Been there before.

Taggart grunted as they carried more than walked Jamison. "Been keepin' a eye on you boys. I reckon I had my own score to settle. Murdock woulda liked that, ya know."

44

THE CLOCK HAD LONG-SINCE STRUCK MIDNIGHT. Two ambulances, uniformed EMTs, half a dozen police officers, three cruisers with their lights flashing, a medical examiner's "bus," and three stretchers carrying body bags containing three corpses, all clustered around Jamison's dark cruiser. It was a three-ring circus in the forest trail off Rutledge Glen Road.

After Travis dropped Brian and Jamison off at the ER, he'd bolted back to the scene. To his surprise, Taggart had not disappeared. He'd asked the old boy to stick around.

Now, Taggart sat on a rotten log looking up at Travis, who rested his right hand on the right shoulder of Taggart's grimy red and black coat— more black than red. And he stunk of deer piss. Travis thought he smelled great.

The old man said, "Din't never see so many guns n' badges 'n crazy lights."

Travis looked down at the old boy, who appeared exhausted, not used to so much excitement, it seemed. He said, "Taggart, I wasn't wearing a vest. Stupid, I know. Bolt probably would have gone through it anyway. You saved my life, old man. I owe you. We'll stop up and visit after this thing is over.

He shook the old man's hand. It was... sticky.

"I'll be waitin'."

SAM'S DIRECT BOSS, LIEUTENANT PAUL O'NEILL, approached. Old Taggart had apparently decided he'd had enough of all this. Travis could imagine him saying that *killin' a man who kilt bears is one thing, but all these badges in one place just ain't natural-like, 'specially in the woods.* He slipped away as quietly as he had entered that campsite earlier.

O'Neill watched the old woodsman shuffle off before turning to Travis and said, "I'm beginning to associate you with dead people, Sam. How 'bout a lift home? "

"Not yet, Lieutenant. With your permission, we have some more business yet tonight—this morning. You and I are going to a warehouse full of goodies after we talk to Jamison."

O'NEILL SHRUGGED, BUT AGREED. TRAVIS WAS determined. One look at his face made that crystal clear.

45

TRAVIS MARCHED INTO JAMISON'S ROOM. A MAN WITH A purpose. Jamison was sitting up with his chest wrapped in white gauze.

"You okay?" Travis thought he looked like hell frozen over.

"X-rays show two cracked ribs, none broken. Pretty sore, but I'll live. How are Kate and Brian?"

"Kate's pretty banged up and Brian is charming the nurses downstairs in the ER. Can I get you anything?"

"Nah, just tell me what's going on."

"O'Neill is getting the warrant drawn up for the warehouse I told you about. I'm going to join him in ten minutes. We've got a team waiting."

Something wasn't being said.

Jamison said, "What's wrong?"

"Do you remember what Hudson said just before he shot you?"

"Something about us thinking we're smarter than him—"

Travis interrupted him, "No, the part about dirt on our badges and being right under our noses. *And* there's the matter of that truck."

Jamison winced as he shifted in the inclined hospital bed.

"What about the truck?"

The phone in the room rang. Travis picked it up. It was O'Neill.

"Yes, Lieutenant. Be right down." He said to Jamison, "Everything's in place. I gotta to go."

Jamison started to crawl out of the bed, but the side rails wouldn't drop.

"Help me—"

"Larry, you can't—"

"Bullshit! I will not be left here. *That's* what can't happen!"

JAMISON LEANED ON TRAVIS. TOGETHER, THEY EMERGED into the hospital lobby from the elevator. O'Neill spotted them through the glass doors as they crossed the almost-empty lobby, exited the hospital and approached his cruiser.

"What the hell is *he* doing here?" He challenged Travis, but stared at Jamison with an expression of surprise and admiration.

Jamison said, "I needn't remind you that you're outranked here, Lieutenant, but I will if I have to. Drive!"

He winced as he dropped into the rear seat of O'Neill's cruiser.

O'Neill bit his tongue. "Yessir!"

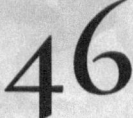

46

Jamison said, "Remember our friend Agent Kim Mason from the U.S. Fish and Wildlife Service, Special Operations, the fed who offered his help and expertise in this case?

"New news: Kate's interview in Chinatown included a photo of the store owner. Mason's mug was in the background, like he owned the place. I'm sure he never realized he was being photographed. What the hell was he doing there?"

Travis nodded. "The poachers traced that supposed 'clean' truck he supplied us back to the U.S. Government motor pool. It looks like Mr. Mason isn't Mr. Clean. Worse, he set us up. O'Neill, get us to the warehouse *fast*. Here's the address. Mason probably already knows about Hudson and his boys, too."

O'NEILL PARKED THE CRUISER ON THE DARKEST PART OF the street that still offered a clear view of the loading dock where Travis and the poachers dropped off their kill just a day earlier.

Travis eyeballed the loading platform with a pair of binoculars. He observed several men loading large pallets into a truck.

He said, "There's our boy," as he handed the binocs to Jamison. "They're rabbiting."

To make matters more interesting, the sky opened up. No lightning, no thunder, just cold rain. A lot of it.

O'NEILL SAID, "EVERYONE IS IN POSITION, CAPTAIN."

Still peering into the binocs and through the sudden downpour, Jamison said, "That limo is leaving. Move in. We'll stay on the limo. *Go!*"

State police, local cops, and O'Neill's men all screeched in toward the warehouse from all directions. Already drenched, Officers in uniform and civilian clothes rushed in on foot from their concealed positions at a quick-step with guns drawn.

They shouted at the warehouse workers, "Police! Stay where you are! Hands where we can see 'em!"

THE MAN INSIDE THE LIMO WATCHED AS THE TAKE-DOWN teams closed in all around. Cops everywhere with guns guarded other cops who ripped open crates with crowbars. Tendrils of smoky vapors rose from dry-iced parts of various animals in containers stenciled "fresh fruit."

Some men were cuffed behind their backs, while they pressed others spread-eagled against a wall and frisked.

The man in the rear of the limo told his driver, "Get us out of here. *Now!*"

O'NEILL'S BLUE STROBE ON THE DASH AND HIS SIREN whooping through now rain-soaked streets brought attention to tires squealing their protest in the still-dry spots under bridges and ramps.

They chased the limo. Both cars slid through

turns and bounced off curbs on the now-slippery streets and alleys.

Sitting in O'Neill's passenger seat with Jamison leaning forward over his left shoulder, Travis said, "Looks like they're headed for the airport."

O'Neill lunged for the dash radio's microphone and said, "Unit two-zero to Dispatch."

"Go ahead, two-zero."

"Send two back-up units to the airport's main gate, *now!*"

"Received, unit two-zero."

47

THE LIMO SCREECHED TO A STOP NEXT TO THE MAIN terminal building. Three Asian men leaped out and grabbed three large suitcases out of the limo's trunk after the driver popped it open from the cockpit. They ran through the terminal doors, lugging their treasure.

O'Neill's unmarked cruiser slammed to a stop as the three suitcase men vanished in the dense crowd inside the terminal building.

Jamison said, "O'Neill, you and one back-up get to the control tower. Make sure nothing takes off.

Send the second one to any gate that has a plane leaving for any Asian country. Also, notify airport security what we're up to. Then check the passenger lists for Oriental names.

Travis snickered, "It'd be just our luck they're headed to Bermuda."

Ignoring the snide remark, O'Neill responded to Jamison's rapid-fire commands. "Got it. Where are you two headed?"

Jamison said, "We'll try a quick scan first. Then hit as many overseas flights as we can. Let's move!"

MASON'S ACCOMPLICES TUCKED THE THREE SUITCASES into three different airport lockers.

They handed him the trio of locker keys. He reached into his pocket and removed an envelope that already had a stamp. With a pen, he jotted an address on the envelope, placed the three keys inside and hurried to a nearby mailbox. He dropped in the envelope.

Mason nodded to each of the men, and all three walked away through the airport's corridors.

THE THREE MEN ROUNDED A CORNER. TRAVIS SPOTTED them. He called to Jamison, who stood a short distance away and nodded toward Mason and his men.

The Asians all rounded a corner, then another even as Travis and Jamison were closing the gap, but then they lost sight of their quarry for a moment. They turned a corner and expected to have closed the gap further, but didn't see them at all. Looked at each other, puzzled.

Out of the corner of his eye, Travis spotted a door marked .

Authorized Personnel Only

The door was still slowly closing. He stuck his foot in the jamb before it automatically locked. Travis drew his revolver as he they entered the secure storage area.

He and Jamison stared up at large shelving units twenty feet high, half-full of boxes, crates, maintenance equipment and spare parts. Travis led. Jamison followed a short distance behind. They split up as they came to two aisles.

Travis peeked around the corner of a large wooden crate when he felt the warm barrel of a pistol poking hard into the back of his head. He froze and set down his own pistol atop the crate at his right shoulder.

A SINGLE SPARK-FILLED CHOP TO THE SIDE OF JAMISON'S neck from behind, and he was awash in dizziness. One grunt later, he dropped to the painted concrete floor. He squinted to focus on his attacker's companion standing over him. He feigned pain and clutched at his neck while he planned his next move.

Still on the floor, Jamison surprised the man behind him by spinning around and taking him down with a fast leg sweep. His attacker went down hard, striking his head on the glossy floor.

The second attacker moved in. Jamison blocked two hand chops and rolled away from a leg stomp. He grabbed that leg and kicked the man square in the groin—still from the floor. Old reliable.

The man crumpled forward. Jamison reached up and chopped his larynx, cutting off his air supply.

Both of his attackers were down, but not out.

WITH TRAVIS STILL HELD AT GUNPOINT BY MASON, HE shoved Travis forward and they came into Jamison's view.

Mason said, "You are indeed skilled in the art, Captain Jamison." He shoved Travis forward again and said to him, "Please join your friend. Both of you sit down... on your hands.

Both officers did as they were told. The two young Asian men, now partially recovered from Jamison's onslaught, joined Mason and his gun.

Travis said with a sneer of disgust, "What now? Kill us too?"

"No. What happened to Murdock was not planned. I had nothing to do with that. I want you to understand how this happened. My people have been using these traditional remedies for over a thousand years."

Jamison wrinkled his brow like he had just smelled shit being served up with fermented piss gravy. "We know. You've plundered your own country of these animals and now you're trying to do the same here."

"In the name of medicine, my friend. You, too, use animals to test perfumes, dyes, make-up, and experiments. So you also violate the creatures you protect."

"It's done within the laws of this land which

ensure their survival. You are nothing more than a fucking thief and a dirty cop."

"My mother is bed ridden with sores and internal ailments that make her cry out night and day. Whether these animals' organs have scientific or medicinal value is of no importance. These remedies soothe and calm her. And many others, as well. My people are poor and uneducated. You have so much. Wouldn't you do the same for your mother?"

Jamison almost shouted, "Spare me all the rationalization, oh wise one. I checked back on all your major cases, Mason. Pretty clever, the way you protected the major dealers and let the little guys hang. Your inside position was perfect to know all the operatives and operations."

Mason just shook his head, waggling his nine millimeter service weapon. "I was told you were good, Jamison. Do not judge me so harshly."

Mason nodded and the two Asians approached Travis and Jamison. Mason reached into his pocket and tossed a pair of handcuffs to one man. They handcuffed the two officers around and behind a metal pipe on the wall. Mason nodded to his comrades and they left.

TRAVIS SAID, "YOU ALL RIGHT, BOSS?"

Jamison was wincing. His cracked ribs, along with the scuffle with the two Kung Fu yo-yos, left him worse for wear.

He smiled and said, "Yeah. We'll run into him again. You still got your portable?"

48

TRAVIS DROPPED JAMISON OFF AT HIS HOUSE—HIS DARK house. After he had closed the front door behind him. Travis drove away.

Jamison limped into the kitchen, turned on a light. Sat on a chair, looked around and sighed. Poured himself a glass of Scotch from the bottle that always sat in the center of the kitchen table these days. He planted his elbows, his head in his hands.

I'm good at my job, aren't I?

TRAVIS MARCHED UP HIS FRONT STAIRS, TRIUMPHANT. HE was still alive. He saw Kate and Brian through the window on their way to greet him. They had heard his victory stomp up onto the porch.

They just huddled on the couch in front of the fireplace in a daze for the longest time, saying nothing. Sam worried about Brian who worried about Kate who worried about Sam.

THE NEXT MORNING, THE PHONE RANG TWICE. TRAVIS picked up. Answered in a gravelly voice still full of sleep. "Yeah, Lar—"

Looked at the clock's face like it was the ugliest thing in his life at that moment. "Uh-huh."

Kate rolled over and cuddled him. He kissed her bruised cheek, still half listening to Jamison on the phone.

"... could've used a few more hours sleep."

He grabbed Kate's hand as she was about to drive him right into utter distraction despite her injuries. Quite a gal.

"Hmmm, I'm willing to play that hunch. Give me a half-hour and I'll pick you up."

Listening to his side of the conversation with Jamison, she said, "What's going on?"

Larry's got an idea. Worth a shot. Gotta go, hon.

I'll keep you posted. You should stay home with Brian and rest.

"Be careful, Travis."

49

O'Neill drove. Jamison and Travis half-faced each other in the back seat.

Jamison spoke of their escaped quarry from the previous night. "Everyone's assumed that they high-tailed it on some plane. I think we bottled things up enough to scare them away from the airport. Maybe they hole up for a while, and *then* move out with the goods."

Travis listened and thought about it. "I like it. Mason knows how we work. So he lays low for a few days until the heat's off. The limo turned up clean... the trick is to figure out where he's hiding."

"How 'bout Chinatown in the city, for starters?"

"Yeah, you could hide a battalion down there, Larry."

"I got another hunch about that, too.

"Why didn't I guess as much, boss?"

TWO HOURS LATER, TRAVIS HAD DRIVEN JAMISON TO THE city. They now sat on Doyers Street in New York's Chinatown with a decent view of the alley that led to the storefront where Kate interviewed Lu Chang.

And so, their stake-out began. They marveled at the hustle and bustle of the Chinese community this early in the day. Wasn't even ten.

Travis's boss squirmed in the passenger seat of his cruiser. He rubbed his left-side rack of ribs with his right hand.

"You are a tough 'ol bastard, Jamison. How sore *are* you?"

"Very. Better get comfy. This could take a while. One thing I've learned through the years. Surveillance is an art form. Patience with every muscle ready to scream into action at a moments notice is absolute."

"Yeah. Not like TV."

. . .

THREE HOURS LATER, TRAVIS HAD JUST DROPPED HIS binoculars into his lap to give his arms a rest. With care, he poked Jamison, who had dozed off. Steered clear of his tenderized ribs.

"Larry! There! The guy you kicked... going into the store. "

Shaking off the fog from his nap, he said, "Okay. Call for some help. Don't use the radio. He may have a scanner trying to monitor our reaction to his escape. No uniforms, marked cruisers, or radio traffic.

After Travis hung up his cell phone, he frowned. "Fifteen minutes, minimum. Should one of us cover the back?"

"We'd stick out like two whores in a convent. Besides, they have no reason to panic and run."

TWO HOURS LATER, THE GUY WAS STILL IN THE STORE somewhere. Lt. O'Neill had raced down to the city. Jamison now sat in the back of another cruiser, speaking to O'Neill and two other officers dressed in civvies.

Jamison said, "In five minutes, at 1200 hours, you three come in through the back. Travis and I will take the front. He might have two friends with him who're good with their hands and feet, so watch it."

FIVE MINUTES AFTER THAT DISCUSSION, TRAVIS AND Jamison entered Lu Chang's store. The old man that Kate interviewed looked harmless enough. He said, "Yes, gentlemen, may I help you?"

"Misters Travis and Jamison for Mr. Mason."

"Ah. But there is no one here by that name."

"Mr. Chang, if you want to stay in business, a little cooperation would go a long way to help you do that."

Travis spotted movement behind a curtain toward the back of the store. He rushed past Lu Chang to give chase. The two Asian men from the airport fled toward the back door to make their escape. As they opened the door, they were confronted by the business-end of the rear-cover officers' semi-automatics—the STOP team, or Special Tactical Operations.

Jamison strolled out the front of the store, leaving a confused Lu Chang standing behind his counter.

With his back against the wall just down the street and around the corner from the shop, Jamison raised his service piece. He counted aloud.

GK JURRENS

"... eight... nine... ten."

He pulled the trigger, murdering an old mattress piled against a stack of wooden pallets. Turned the corner to move back to the front of the store. And he confronted a very surprised Special Agent Mason, just about to clear the storefront's doorway after hearing what sounded like a distant gunshot.

"You're under arrest, Mason." Jamison made sure his expression left no doubt. If Mason resisted, he *would* shoot his corrupt ass.

262

50

MASON AND HIS TWO KUNG FU STOOGES WERE ALL handcuffed and surrounded by four uniformed officers, Jamison, Travis and O'Neill.

The entire herd marched down a hall and turned into a door marked Superior Court. It was a large room with pictures of past-presiding justices, a corralled-off jury box, a prisoner's docket and rows of law books from floor to ceiling on one wall.

Mason addressed Jamison with his hands still cuffed behind his back. "Can I make my phone call now? Can you take these off?"

Travis said, "Not entirely."

He unlocked Mason's right hand, walked him to a handcuff rail and secured his right wrist to it.

Still collected and under control, Mason accepted the phone from Travis, who continued to watch him with his favorite stink-eye. Mason dialed. His voice was barely audible. He completed his call and sat next to the cuff rail with which he was getting acquainted.

Assistant District Attorney Peter Dunwoody entered the room trailing smoke behind him from his ever-present cigarette and grim smirk. He'd represent the state. He nodded all around, with a sideways glance at the three cuffed prisoners. He'd never laid eyes on any of them before.

Jamison hunkered down with Dunwoody for a few minutes before they turned and faced Travis.

Jamison said, "Sam, please work with Peter here," a respectful nod to the prosecutor for the state, "to start the paperwork and draw up the charges. The judge will be in straightaway."

Mason said, "I should tell you that you needn't bother. This matter will be cleared up in short order."

Jamison didn't like the man's tone of voice, like Mason was privy to something he wasn't. But he wouldn't give the prick the satisfaction.

"Yeah, about twenty years in one of your own crossbar hotels, Mason."

Dunwoody cast his gaze downward as if he knew, or at least suspected, what was coming. But he placed a paternal hand on Sam's shoulder, and the two left the room. Dunwoody muttered something to Sam, but Jamison couldn't hear.

Ten minutes later, the door opened. In strolled an impeccably tailored three-piece charcoal suit, a powder-blue shirt with a board-stiff white collar that blinded the eye and could break bricks. The French cuffs displayed diamond links along with the well-groomed man inside all that finery. All eyes were riveted to this splendid display of costly haber-dashery. Dunwoody and Travis had apparently observed his approach from the hallway, and followed him in.

"Good afternoon, gentlemen. I'm Deputy U.S. Attorney Richard Lowry. Here are my credentials along with a writ you'll want to examine."

After admiring that suit, Jamison first stared Lowry in the eye and then scoured his proffered ID.

The writ, signed by a federal judge, ordered Mason's release.

Dunwoody approached Jamison who shoved the writ in his direction.

Picking up on an atmosphere of skepticism, Lowry said, "Please feel free to call my office if you have questions."

Jamison nodded to O'Neill, who picked up a phone book, located a number, dialed the phone near where the court recorder would sit.

Meanwhile, with Dunwoody looking on over the top of his glasses, Lowry said, "This man, Special Agent Mason, employed by the U.S. Fish and Wildlife Service, is on special assignment to the Department of Justice."

"I'm Captain Jamison of the Massachusetts Environmental Police. And this is—"

Lowry interrupted. "No need for an introduction. Mr. Dunwoody and I have crossed paths."

"With all due respect, Mr. Lowry, Special Agent Mason will be charged with conspiracy, accessory to murder, illegal trafficking of endangered species, and a list of other offenses we haven't yet compiled."

"Captain Jamison, this must be difficult for you to accept; however, Special Agent Mason has been working undercover for the express purpose of determining the numbers, methods, and extent of illegal wildlife commercialization here in the northeast.

Jamison scoffed. "He's dirty and we're going to prove it."

"Captain, if you can answer *yes* to any of the following questions, I will listen to a rebuttal. Did you observe, hear or tape any conversation involving Special Agent Mason, which has the elements of conspiracy or murder?"

Jamison stared at Lowry, but said nothing. Dunwoody continued to study the writ with a critical eye.

"Did you see Special Agent Mason engage in wildlife trafficking not authorized by his statutory powers?"

Jamison still said nothing. But he would not release Lowry from his stare, bordering on incredulity.

"Did you witness any illegal activity conducted by Special Agent Mason that involved unlawful monetary transactions, to wit, keeping contraband for his personal gain or profit?"

More silence.

"Did Special Agent Mason act in any unauthorized manner with firearms or weapons other than protecting his covert identity and self defense?

"Mr. Mason, in fact, is under no obligation to

divulge to you any of his activity, intelligence gathering, or transactions. Therefore, whatever you saw,
or thought you saw, was legitimate activity authorized by the Federal Government which, by the way,
supersedes any Commonwealth of Massachusetts
interests.

Jamison started rubbing his ribs again. He knew
damn well that mean-eyed Hudson worked for
Mason and had shot him. Finally, he glanced to his
right toward Dunwoody who still would not look up
to meet his gaze. Apparently, he was on his own.

"Captain Jamison, release Mr. Mason to my
custody forthwith."

Fuck!

Dunwoody looked up. He looked at Jamison and
said with sad eyes, "It's legit. You must release
Mason into Mr. Lowry's custody. But per your writ,
the court officers can hold these other two men for
assaulting officers of the law."

Jamison was savvy enough to know he needed to
survive to lock up this Mason prick another day. Or
plant a nine-mil slug between his eyes.

Travis had dropped his jaw. It stayed there, until
he growled, "What the hell is this?"

Jamison said, "Release Mason."

"*What?*"

Jamison worried Travis would do something stupid. "The U.S. Attorney says so. I'll explain later."

"Like hell I will! This son-of-a-bitch nearly killed me!"

Jamison whispered into Travis's right ear, "Sam, please. We have no choice." Dunwoody also nodded to Travis.

AFTER TURNING THE TWO KOREAN'S OVER TO THE CUSTODY of the local sheriff so they could be held over for arraignment, Jamison and Travis trudged out of the courtroom and down the courthouse steps, numb and disbelieving. They stopped at their cruiser. Across the street, Mason shook Lowry's hand, and they both slid into the back of a limo.

"We did a good job, Sam. Round one goes to them. We'll be better prepared for the next one."

"So will they, Larry."

"Don't worry, partner, I have a few ideas. This guy's guilty, and we're going to prove it."

Sam had never seen such expression on the face of his boss's boss—somewhere between mischievous and conspiratorial.

A beat later, Sam grinned, too.

51

BACK OUT AT THE NOW-DEAD POACHERS' CAMP, TWO black bears—a sow and her cub—approached the site with caution, sniffing the air and testing it for danger.

Their curiosity turned into the unending search for food.

Within minutes, they had demolished the camp. Tents flattened and shredded, cans and foodstuffs torn open and eaten.

A crisp breeze rippled through the ebony cub's

glistening coat. Its dark and mischievous eyes sparkled in the reflected light from Sunrise Lake.

Then the faint sound of baying hounds in the distance grew louder. In a sudden panic, the sow emitted a low growl and the two bears lumbered away into the forest.

The End?
Not by a long shot!

CAST OF MAJOR CHARACTERS

- **Russell (Russ) Baker:** Sam Travis's undercover alias.
- **Lu Chang:** Proprietor of an exotic shop in the alley off Doyers Street in New York City's Chinatown
- **Peter Dunwoody**: Assistant District Attorney of the Commonwealth of Massachusetts.
- **Charles M. (Charlie) Hudson**: Lead poacher
- **Captain Lawrence R. (Larry) Jamison**: Commandant of the Massachusetts Environmental Police Academy and Sam Travis's temporary partner.
- **Richard Lowry:** US Federal Assistant District Attorney (AUSA)

- **Kim Mason:** A covert U.S. Fish and Wildlife Service agent, Special Operations.
- **Anthony R. (Tony) McRae**: A member of Hudson's poaching team.
- **Katherine (Kate) Miller:** Wedgewood Courier's investigative reporter and Sam Travis's girlfriend.
- **Frank Murdock:** Murder victim and Sam Travis's long-time partner
- **Judy Murdock:** Frank Murdock's surviving widow.
- **Lieutenant Paul O'Neill:** Sam Travis's direct boss at the Massachusetts Environment Police Department.
- **Randall (Randy) Sackett**: A member of Hudson's poaching team and ex-professional wrestler.
- **Silas Taggart**: Mountain man who befriended Frank Murdock before he was killed.
- **Brian Travis**: Son of Sam Travis.
- **Samuel (Sam) Travis**: A Massachusetts Environmental Police Officer. EPOs in the Commonwealth of Massachusetts possess wide-ranging authority as a separate law enforcement agency with

full statutory police power throughout the state. EPOs exercise broad search and seizure powers unlike other police agencies.

- **Thomas I. (Tom) Verdi**: Commissioner of the Massachusetts Environmental Police Department

OTHER BOOKS BY GK JURRENS

Historical Fiction (Great Depression Era Crime)

- **Black Blizzard: A Lyon County Adventure**
- **Murder in Purgatory: A Lyon County Mystery**

Aubrey Greigh Mysteries

- **Voodoo Vendetta - Culture That Kills**
- **Dancing With Death - Who Will Die? Or Disappear?**

Sam Travis Adventures:

- **Lethal Game - Bears Under Siege**

Contemporary Autobiographical Fiction (Drama)

- **Dangerous Dreams: Dream Runners: Book 1**

- **Fractured Dreams: Dream Runners: Book 2**

Futuristic Fiction (Paranormal Mystery Thrillers)

- **Underground, Mayhem: Book 1**
- **Mean Streets, Mayhem: Book 2**
- **Post Earth, Mayhem: Book 3**
- **A Glimpse of Mayhem: Companion Guide to the Mayhem Trilogy**

Non-fiction

- **The Poetic Detective: Investigate Rhyme With Reason**
- **Why Write? Why Publish? Passion? Profit? Both?**
- **Moving a Boat and Her Crew**
- **Restoring a Boat and Her Crew**

Turn the page to read an excerpt from Gene's new book:
Dancing With Death - Who Will Die? Or Disappear?

EXCERPT FROM DANCING WITH DEATH

AN AUBREY GREIGH MYSTERY

Late Evening
Monday, August 10th
City Lux Executive Apartments
Suite 3-16
9 Tietgensgade
Kobenhavn (Copenhagen), Denmark

Shite! Something is very wrong....

The thought prickled Aubrey Greigh's every nerve ending. In contrast to the warm hallway, a chill breeze funneled through the crack between the lavish suite's entry door and its jamb.

Not good, the door ajar.

He whispered another curse as he stood with his

Monday, August 10th

back to the opulent hall. A gust of cold air caused a momentary whistle as it puffed out from inside the suite. His skin crawled as goosebumps sprouted all over his body, confirming his fear that something indeed had gone very wrong.

On instant alert, he peeked in and eased open the door with one knuckle, his face a mask of concentration; if he carried a gun, it would have been out in front, held low and ready. Not a master of mixed martial arts, but Greigh managed to take care of himself in a fight better than most.

"Peter?" Nothing. Louder. The same.

He had expected Peter Fontera to meet him at the door, flashing his dazzling white dental implants. He was a force of nature at any gathering; a man who elicited both admiration and exasperation with his quirks. A likable bloke.

Greigh had never been here before. As he stepped into the suite, a rental, he noticed a portrait in the dim light of the foyer - a framed headshot on the only table. It was as though someone had placed it there with deliberation, to catch the bright recessed spot overhead. The whole room was lit with a dim glow by that single light focused on that one picture.

The atmosphere of the place felt eerie and uncomfortable. Greigh struggled to identify why.

Something about that photo unsettled him. And the silence. He couldn't wait to leave.

That portrait—an oil painting?—was small enough to fit into a suitcase, but large enough to broadcast professional vanity. It featured the tools of Peter's trade: a Botox'd face and perfect hair. His movie-star smile and dimpled chin hovered over a wild bowtie. The light achieved its purpose at just the right angle.

Peter was famous for those hideous bowties. Even the characters he portrayed in every movie all wore them. The entertainment media loved to report that those ties were the subject of an ironclad provision in his every contract. Made him appear a tad wonky. Only Peter could pull it off.

Greigh didn't care. Didn't know him, other than as a source. Most said Fontera was the nicest bloke ever. Greigh allowed his set of ever-present antique brass knuckles gripped in his right hand and a small but powerful flashlight in his left guide him.

And there he sprawled.

Stunned, Greigh tracked through a spreading pool of blood that surrounded the international celebrity who now lay at his feet. Peter appeared either already dead or close to it.

The body was unrecognizable except for that silly tie. Greigh's stomach flipped. But he had already envisioned this horrific scene. In his mind's eye. Didn't make it any easier. He swallowed hard. Mopped his brow.

Sweating despite this cool breeze? To business, then.

The night air caused the white curtains to billow inward at the balcony's French doors open wide to the starry sky and the heavens. A sign of earthly surrender?

How bloody poetic....

Before tonight, everyone in the western hemisphere would have recognized Peter Fontera from stage and screen. His popularity had soared as the most prominent Chicago studios satisfied a sudden retro demand. Windy City Productions led the way with stars like Peter Fontera and Stacy Michaels.

A few years ago, the public once again hungered for skilled human actors and real-world settings in their entertainment, versus the industry standard—those that were computer generated or enhanced. CG—a.k.a. CGI—had been all the rage for decades. It got old. Greigh agreed.

So handsome in life, Peter now seemed artificial. He was still alive, wasn't he? Or was that just incorrigible optimism? Though repulsed by violent and messy death, Greigh went to work.

All right, then. Pulse at carotid? Indiscernible. At femoral artery? Almost non-existent. Check. Mouth-to-mouth? Out of the question. Not much left of the poor bastard's face. Like that was one of the killer's targets. No killing wound there. But no chance for a controlled airway. Chest compressions, it is.

These high-velocity thoughts swirled like dust devils through Greigh's parched consciousness, along with the gruesome sight of Peter's exposed crotch area that had been reduced to soupy kibble.

Bloody hell!

Another gut lurch. He focused on Peter's chest. Straightaway, he started cracking Fontera's rib and sternum cartilage a hundred times per minute until he realized it was all too little, too late. He kept going. No stranger to violence, Greigh nevertheless abhorred it.

With Fontera's blood and other fluids everywhere, including all over Greigh's own hands, arms, knees, and the soles of his sandals, he discarded any concern over leaving fingerprints and distinctive tracks. Couldn't be helped. He had not worn gloves, much less waders. He did not expect to slog through a bloodbath and drop to his hands and knees into the thick of it.

After less than two minutes, he gave up, already huffing like he'd run a race. Most can't appreciate the exertion proper chest compressions require. He mopped his sweaty brow.

Did I just smear this poor blighter's blood all over my forehead? Shite! What had Peter learned that he'll now take with him to his grave?

A week earlier, Interpol contacted Greigh as he ate breakfast in his suite at the Hotel Literati in Chicago's Near Southwest Loop. His presence was required in Denmark within twelve hours. Unprecedented. Until now, he did the contacting.

And he'd be traveling incognito. False papers—passport, international driver's license and credit cards, deep background with a clean criminal history—the works. It would all be waiting in a locker at O'Hare, they said. This was also new. Nobody creates a complete legend—a deep cover identity—in twelve hours. Pre-meditated, then. Interesting. He'd talk to Freya about that.

Now, he stood in a murdered man's apartment.

Earlier today, Peter Fontera had contacted him. Under his cover, Greigh posed as an entertainment reporter covering the latest Windy City movie project, *Dancing With Death*. He'd shared coffee with the actor at the waterfront set the last few days during breaks in the shooting. They'd hit it off—two creatives.

Tonight, not knowing who to trust, Peter said he had vital information to share, but only with Greigh. Too little, too late. Tonight's theme, apparently.

Greigh liked the lanky but dashing fellow. He cursed himself for burning two precious minutes administering useless chest compressions to a corpse.

Even under less dismal conditions, he knew the average failure statistics behind cardiopulmonary resuscitation. Here and now, they were *far* worse than that. There was always room for hope until... there wasn't. That time had come and gone.

Well, then, right so! Face obliterated, chest wound still pumping, but... no defensive wounds? Unconscious, unresponsive. Shite be on the saints!

Time passed Greigh by in a fog of futile optimism—his Kryptonite. Now, the police couldn't be far. After failing to raise a pulse, Greigh got to his feet. Almost slipped and fell in the wet mess. Even his toes stuck together in a stinky soup. He'd worn his *thinking sandals* despite the nip in the air. If only he'd known....

Time to beat a hasty retreat. The team would sort all the rest later. He turned to bolt out of the suite's door on the sixteenth floor of the ultra-contemporary City Lux condos. No sooner had he crossed the threshold than a gazillion-candlepower beam stunned him..

"Hænder, hvor jeg kan se dem. Nu!"

Bloody brilliant! Just what I need.

Greigh's working knowledge of Danish made it clear the cop had said, "Hands where I can see them. Now!"

He complied. No sudden moves. Not now. Street cops in any country made his left eye tick. The voice behind the light reported over comms. Translating in his head, "One in custody."

Four rough hands shoved him face-first against the wall to his immediate right, in the hallway just outside the suite. Not his first rodeo, as the Yanks might say.

Three other tactical-clad human tanks slid by to clear the rest of the massive suite with their artillery at the ready.

Who had called them in? Were these lads the Lux's concierge cops? Nope, these boys were Tactical Squad— or whatever they called them here. Copenhagen's finest.

From deeper inside the apartment, one cop said,

"Body!" And then three seconds later, a shout of, "Clear!" Then one more. A softer voice, likely the first bugger again, and almost inaudible from the hallway, the bloke spoke with, what? Horrific awe? His response translated to "Holy Mother of God...."

Yup. That was the first one who discovered Peter's remains. Is that wanker now vomiting in their crime scene? Sure sounds like it. A tank with a sensitive gut? Bloody hell. Must be a rookie. One of the Tacs? That is, a member of the highly-trained tactical squad of the Chicago Enforcement Department? This isn't Chicago!

Before even being told to do so, Greigh piled both palms on top of his head, leaving two smeared handprints on the wall in front of his face.

Two hands—not his—turned out his pockets, while two more held a compact H&K 9mm pistol to his left temple in a white-knuckled grip. They discovered his wallet, US passport, and a few Danish and American bills clipped together.

They dug deeper for some loose change, an A-bus pass, a folding knife, and a small flashlight. He winced. The officer handling him bruised the boys— the family jewels—exploring the depths of his jeans' front pockets, perhaps rooting out some dangerous lint.

Bollocks!

Greigh stared at his own shadow.

It stared back at him from the lavender wall, an inch from his nose. The cop-strength body spot lit his backside with his hands still on his head. Not his best pose for the official body cam recording. His elevated elbows gave his sharp-edged shadow a shape that reminded him of a bird of prey.

Someone bloody well preyed on poor Peter tonight.

Greigh heard the cuffs clink as they snicked away from an equipment belt behind him. He anticipated the need to bring his right hand down to get hooked up. But not so soon or so fast that the arresting officer would think he was making an offensive move.

He swung his arm out to his side in a slow, wide arc, always keeping his hand open and visible, until it was low enough. With one hand now cuffed—pinch-tight—he lowered his open left palm behind his back in the same fashion.

After pinning him harder against the wall, the cop grunted the Danish equivalent of an appreciative, "Huh," like it was a relief dealing with a professional. Textbook hook-up. But the poor fellow's breath broadcast yesterday's garlic. Caused Greigh's stomach to lurch. Again. More jarring.

He'd bet this edgy officer was likely into his second or third shift in a row. The guy could use a change of uniform and a shower. Bad breath and BO —the universal labor language.

Exhausting, all this scurrying about. Most trying. And tedious.

One officer read the Danish equivalent of Greigh's rights to him. Since Greigh had yet to utter a single syllable, they still assumed he was a local, despite the passport.

Hmmm... they're not as sharp as I thought. Or....

Another human tank escorted him out to a waiting paddy wagon, a high-security panel van out on Tietgensgade. Looked like they assumed he was a very dangerous guy—like an airborne tornado biding its time to drop from the clouds and strike without warning. If they only knew....

It was mighty uncomfortable to be so wet and sticky. He was a mess, face to feet, stinking like yesterday's sewage. Like he'd been rolling in the stuff. Not just blood, either.

Smart cops. They'd thrown a plastic sheet over the seat toward which he was being guided in no uncertain terms. They forced him down onto a bench in the van's cage toward its rear door on the driver's side. The doors remained open.

After a while, old blood ripens and reeks before it scabs or scales. And that's just the blood. Even rugged Naugahyde upholstery is not immune. Not even this snazzy Volvo EV van—high security law enforcement edition.

They seemed to have sent the first string—except for the projectile vomiter. Nothing but the best for the suspected killer of a celebrity victim—McQ would call poor Peter a *vic*.

———

Tietgensgade Boulevard
    Kobenhavn (Copenhagen), Denmark

A battalion of vultures already flocked in force, even this late on a Monday night. Must be a slow news day.

By the time the tac squad led Greigh out for his walk of shame, the night burned brilliantly from all the spotlights out on the Tietgensgade.

Serious battery power pushed megawatts out there. They dappled the caravan of police cruisers and "his" van-slash-mobile cell in high-contrast through the dried leaves that still clung to the trees lining this exclusive neighborhood's sidewalks.

A veritable media circus had already set up behind the portable barricades beyond the Lux's circle drive. Felt like an old-fashioned movie premier in Old Hollywood. Somehow, the media always got the word, almost before the cops.

This might be a brilliant scene for a reality series called "Star Killers."

But the *Men in Black* surprised Greigh. He smiled at his private quip.

He spotted the pair of suits near the van's still-open rear doors. His sharp eyes zeroed in on tiny lapel pins adorning these two well-tailored hulks. Each bore a white cross on a field of red with a gold border. Hard to miss on those custom-fit charcoal suit coats.

DDIS agents? Their international colleagues referred to them as the Danish Defence Intelligence Service. After all, who in bloody hell accurately pronounced their agency's real moniker in Danish —*Forsvarets Efterretningstjeneste*. Or who'd remember what the acronym *FE* meant? The agency was enigmatic enough to be known by other names, too.

Greigh researched a past manuscript, one of his earlier novels. Plus, he'd spent time in Denmark. He learned that DDIS responsibilities included collecting information about national political, financial, scientific, and military interests. Maybe even UFOs.

So, why on Earth would DDIS be interested in a common homicide—even that of a celebrity? What might they know that he didn't? Most curious.

He'd ask Freya Ecklund, his handler.

Fontera had been in Copenhagen for the last three weeks on location for his starring role in *Dancing With Death*. Although he couldn't have foreseen *this* scene as his finale.

And nobody had captured the murder on video. That cold-hearted prig of a producer would no doubt lament *that* more than his star's violent demise.

Celebrity victims always nipped the best coverage—especially homicides with a salacious theme. And if that theme involved a bizarre modus operandi? Even juicier.

Was this personal vengeance, or something else?

Greigh worried about the news crews. He hoped they were far enough away....

Vultures have a job to do, too, I suppose. The same everywhere. Nobody recognizes me. So far, at least.

Greigh kept his head lowered, just the same. Why on earth had Interpol asked him to travel under a false identity this time? Made no sense. If anyone recognized him, he'd be famous for yet another reason. He chastised himself.

Bloody brilliant, this.

Greigh could not afford such exposure. He imagined his publisher stroking out. Besides, all of this was inconsistent with the damn mission.

And he had screwed up. Stupid to attempt triage with that much blood loss and soft tissue damage. Had to try, didn't he? Precious minutes lost needed to make his escape. A leopard can't change his stripes, as they say. Or some such rot.

American idioms!

There'd be hell to pay, and he'd be the one paying. But these cops were the least of his worries. He'd try not to think about all of this until after they cleaned him up. If he was lucky, they'd subject him to a good night's rest in a holding cell, and possibly even a state-sponsored breakfast. He hadn't eaten or slept since, what, yesterday?

Shite!

Not easy to switch off the mind of an investigator. Despite his best efforts to do so, Greigh reflected during his bumpy van ride to Tårnby—he'd heard the driver mention their destination while he chatted with his dispatcher.

Greigh imagined the dead guy's luxury rental suite before all the blood on the floor, damaged walls, ceiling and furnishings, not to mention the contents of Peter's vacated bladder and colon.

Someone had rented that apartment almost a month ago for this star of stage and screen. It was every bit as spectacular as his famous high-rise on the *Mag Mile* back in Chicago. That's what the locals called it—Mag was short for Magnificent. They called it that or the *Miracle Mile*—a bunch of over-priced apartment buildings and concierge busi-nesses inside the West Loop. That patch was once quite the tourist trap.

The best apartments boasted the most splendid lake views. But Fontera preferred the river side. They "re-gentrified" that entire area on the Chicago River about twenty years ago so they could justify the "exclusive"—that is, bloody inflated—prices for that rarified real estate.

These days, most stars and other celebrities huddled near each other on Celebrity Row out at the southeastern shore of Lake Michigan. That portion of Chicago—the city now a massive regionplex of fifty million souls—was recently part of Western Indiana before bored politicians redrew invisible lines. The lake now stunk like shite, but... it *was* lake shore.

Everyone said "The Row" made the Hollywood Hills look like a shantytown by comparison. They even featured their own mag-lev limo train from out there into all the major studio lots north of the Cicero district. And the rolling parties between The Row and Cicero were the stuff of legends.

No doubt Fontera's suite on the Mag Mile, as well as his mansion out on The Row, would fall to his heirs, if he had any.

Shite-for-brains idiots with money. I'm different, though... aren't I?

Fontera never had a chance, the poor sod.

In the few minutes Greigh had been in the celebrity's suite near Copenhagen's city center, he concluded the killer was not a professional. Too messy. Too personal. Or it was just meant to appear that way, as if someone was sending a message? A brutal one.

It appeared the movie star had expired from exsanguination. Greigh's cop friend in Chicago—the lovely Detective Chance McQuillan, a.k.a. McQ—would say he "bled out."

A pro hitter would have delivered one or more decisive insurance strikes—two or more in the chest, one in the head or face—just to make sure. But it appeared the killer's blade hit no vital organs. Sloppy, unless... for appearances....

Greigh speculated Fontera might even have still been alive as the killer fled. *He'd* assumed so, hadn't he? It's possible he even interrupted the kill. And that would beg the question of how he missed the murderer.

Further, Peter's door was open when Greigh arrived. No evidence of forced entry. And this high-end apartment featured a sophisticated security system with a video monitor. Peter knew his killer and had let him or her in. He'd pass all this info on to Freya at his earliest opportunity. And possibly to the local police at the appropriate time.

They sat in the Tårnby station.

The veteran street cop with the bad breath and body odor sat behind a small steel desk with chipped corners and dented sides. He stared at Greigh's passport. Still covered in drying blood from head to every toe—no doubt that was by design—Greigh squirmed in the bolted-down guest chair with his right hand cuffed to its frame. The cop must have construed his squirming as post-homicidal jitters.

Tac guys doubling as intake processors? Interesting. Not Chicago, for sure.

This squad room, though smaller, vibed very much like McQ's at the ninety-ninth precinct house back in Chicago. Before they placed her on administrative leave for getting a civilian killed, like McQ's squad, this one stunk of burnt coffee... and something more foul. Like week-old sweat socks.

He glanced up at the stained ceiling. Lots of dents and holes in the acoustic tile, like this guy's desk, only more holes than dents. Under his feet, most floor tiles had long ago defeated their underlying adhesive and lost their corners.

Raucous dregs of humanity acted out minor flurries of boisterous drama all around them.

Yup, much like the nine-nine.

Officer Halitosis said in accented English lilting with some volume over the din, "So, Mr. Arthur Granville, is it? What kind of name is that?"

The very Scottish Aubrey Greigh said, "Irish, laddy. Grew up there. Now a naturalized American citizen, proud to say. Dual citizenship."

"So, Mr. Granville, why did you kill him? Mr. Fontera?"

"What say you just process me in, Officer? I'd be delighted to chat with your detectives."

"You'll then be spending the night in a holding cell, røvhul." Greigh knew that was the Danish version of smart-arse—paraphrased for polite company.

"'That'll be quite alright. What are your meal options down there, boyo?"

Even the Danes allowed those incarcerated one phone call.

"Freya, a complication in the mission plan, dear. I'm calling from Tårnby station. Fontera is dead. It was personal, not a hit. Or at least meant to appear that way. I'm a suspect and in custody."

"Keep your mouth shut and sit tight."

He just adored his Interpol handler's accent—less lilt, more growl.

And he loved her black American Express Card even more.

ABOUT THE AUTHOR

GK Jurrens writes with undiluted passion, having published a dozen fiction and non-fiction titles to date including ten novels. He also teaches writing and independent publishing nationwide.

GK and his wife live and travel in a motorhome. They wander their beloved North America as a source of endless inspiration.

After studying Liberal Arts and Electronics Engineering Technology, GK earned a Bachelor of Science degree in Business and a Master of Science degree in Management of Technology from the University of Minnesota, USA.

Six years of government service and a successful three-decade career in global high-technology preceded more than a few years of sailing America's waterways, the Florida Keys, and the Eastern Caribbean from the British Virgin Islands to Granada, near the coasts of Venezuela and Trinidad. And brief forays sailing around the Greek Cyclades

Islands in the Aegean Sea and the San Juan Islands in the American Pacific Northwest.

GK now pursues his life-long penchant for the creative arts: prose and poetry, painting (watercolor), traveling (North America), playing guitar and his growing collection of Native American style flutes, some of which he crafted while living in the Arizona desert.

He enjoys quiet evenings reading and exploring movies, when not writing or sitting by a campfire alongside his copilot and soulmate of over half a century—'Admiral' Kay.

If you'd care to offer the author feedback, for which he'd be grateful, consider emailing **gjurrens@yahoo.com** or visit **GKJurrens.com** and subscribe.

ABOUT TOM KASPRZAK
THE REAL SAM TRAVIS

"LT" spent thirty-two years as an environmental police officer for the Commonwealth of Massachusetts. Before graduating in 1977 from the Massachusetts State Police academy, Tom earned the coveted "top gun" award for superior marksmanship.

He began his EPO career as a field officer in various assignments involving both inland and marine enforcement in places like Cape Cod, Boston Harbor and others. After transferring to the Berkshire Mountains in Western Massachusetts with skills honed from 7+ years of varied case involvement and courtroom testimony, he forged close relationships with local and state police.

Upon being promoted to lieutenant, he led a region of officers in search and rescue operations involving plane crashes, boating fatalities, narcotics, and the investigation and apprehension of various firearm violators.

Beginning in 1986, LT engaged in undercover or

supervised undercover operations focused on endangered wildlife. During that time, he worked with other local, state, and federal agencies on issues ranging from the environment to anti-terrorism.

Tom was selected to train in no fewer than three extended tours at the prestigious Federal Law Enforcement Training Center (FLETC) in Glynco, Georgia, where federal law enforcement agencies train.

Those intensive and immersive training tours honed his skills for inter-agency undercover operations, marine operations, and advanced operational readiness. He also trained for, and was an Incident Commander in several cases.

During his colorful career, Tom worked with the Massachusetts State Police air wing on helicopter operations, their dive team, apprehension team, marine law enforcement, and environmental police operations.

Tom spent his last seven years assigned to the State Police STOP (apprehension) team headquarters in Chicopee, Massachusetts, along with all the members of the region he supervised.

His undercover assignments brought dozens of individuals to justice who violated state and federal laws. He was also a Deputy National Marine Fisheries agent as well as a U.S Deputy Fish and Wildlife agent at the same time.

His largest case—Operation Berkshire—closed one of the country's largest illegal commercial wildlife trafficking operations involving twenty-nine individuals, six states and two foreign countries.

The exploits of Tom and his fellow officers from his home state and others led to new exploits in crusading against illegal wildlife commercialization.

National Geographic produced a special called "Wildlife Wars: Bears Under Siege" that featured Tom and his fellow undercover operatives after they closed Operation Berkshire.

Tom taught new recruits at the State Police Academy courses in courtroom procedures, officer ethics and undercover operations. He also delivered endangered species lectures to schools, colleges, municipal police departments, as well as to other state and federal agencies including US Coast Guard District One in Boston with whom he was specifically trained in LNG (Liquid Natural Gas) tanker escort anti-terrorism protocols in Boston Harbor.

He made a name for himself during dozens of successful missing persons, body recovery cases, undercover operations, anti-terrorism and crime scene investigations. Tom and his life partner, Karen, now split their time between Western Massachusetts and Southwestern Florida.